ALL THE WAYS A HEART BURNS

A Voyage YA Anthology

ALL THE WAYS A HEART BURNS

A Voyage YA Anthology

Edited by
Racquel Henry
Marquita Hockaday
and Kip Wilson

Published by *Voyage YA by Uncharted*. *Voyage YA by Uncharted* is an online literary magazine published biweekly.

ISBN 979-8-9882557-4-1

Book interior by Julianne Johnson.
Cover by Emelie Mano.

Content Warning: mentions of suicidal ideation, depression, self-harm, brief descriptions of death and blood, off-page death of a teenager.

WATCHING PAINT DRY

Aaron H. Aceves

"Have you picked a color yet, mijo?"

"No," I reply, making my way across the living room to where my mom is sitting on the couch.

"I want this one," she says, picking up a glittery red nail polish from the wooden coffee table. It's one of a dozen or so bottles displayed there. "See how easy that was?"

I sigh as I sit down next to her. "Picking a nail color isn't as a big of a commitment as choosing a room color, Mom."

"Ay, we could always paint it another color if you get tired of it. Just make a decision already, Adam!"

I don't say anything as I take the nail polish from her. We went to Home Depot a few days ago and I saw how much paint costs. It absolutely doesn't make any sense, but it's expensive as fuck. And there's no way I'm making her pay for it more than once considering how much this new apartment is per month (even though it's a one-bedroom, which means she sleeps in the living room).

"Do you like it?" my mom asks as I unscrew the top of the bottle.

"Of course I do. I bought it."

"But a long time ago, I'm assuming? It's almost empty."

"No. Not even a year ago."

"Oh, so you must like it a lot then."

I nod. "It reminds me of Dorothy's slippers in *The Wizard of Oz*."

My mom beams at me, and I think about how if my dad were here, he'd say something about how what I said was super fucking gay. But it's not like I ever would have talked openly about my love of nail polish if he were here.

"Okay, gimme your hand," I say.

My mom's already removed her last polish, a Christmasy green that had no business being worn in July. But the woman wants what she wants, and today she wants Ruby Slipper Glam.

After I apply a base coat, my first stroke with the red is down the middle of her nail. My second splays the brush to one side and my third sweeps it across the other. A couple more strokes to blend and just like that the first coat is done.

"Wow," Mom says. "I'll never get over how good you are at that. Maybe you'll be a surgeon one day."

Once again, my response is silence. My dream isn't cutting people open no matter how proud that would make my mom. Instead, I move on to the next nail.

When my job is done, Mom gently blows on her fingers, and we settle in for a marathon of our favorite TV show, *Impractical Jokers*. It's this prank show where four guys take turns being told what to do by the other three. My dad used to like it too, but for the past few weeks, I've been doing my best not to think of him when we watch it.

"Who's that?" Mom asks when my phone buzzes for the fourth time in my pocket.

"Probably Noe. He got back from his family vacation yesterday, and I'm guessing he wants to hang."

"Why don't you go? You haven't seen him in a while."

That's been on purpose. Even before he left for his trip, I managed not to see him by claiming to be sick or busy. I don't want to tell him about everything that's gone down. Especially because there's a key bit of information he'd need for it all to make sense, and I'm absolutely not ready to reveal it to him.

"He's a lot, Mom. You know this."

"You like that he's a lot. You have for ten years."

"I know… I just… I'd rather be here, okay?"

"Okay." She looks like she wants to say more, but all she does is say it again. "Okay."

THE NEXT NIGHT, MOM AND I find ourselves on the couch again watching TV. I do my own nails this time. Black with a matte finish. I don't need to do as many coats this time because it's not a glitter polish.

"They're nice," Mom says.

I nod. They're okay. The only reason I chose this color is the fact that I can wear it in public, and as long as I act as straight as the goth guys who wear it, I should be fine. I don't really have an emo look, but I do tend to wear all black just because it's slimming.

"What time is Noe picking you up?"

"At nine," I say.

He finally wore me down. Earlier today, I begrudgingly agreed to go to a party with him. It's not that I don't like parties; it's that I don't like how Noe acts at parties. He cares too much what everyone thinks about him, and sometimes that means I become the butt of his jokes when he's trying to impress people. But that's not always the case, and he really is a good friend. Sometimes. So it's fine. Plus, it's not like I have a choice. Once he calls and I hear his familiar East LA accent, I can't say no. Even when all he's talking about is how "it's gonna be so fucking lit, foo," and how he's gonna get "fucking smashed," I still can't say no.

"From here?" Mom asks.

"No. I told him to pick me up from the burger place around the corner."

Again, I can't explain why we moved without telling him all the other stuff too.

"Oh. Well. Be good. Be safe."

"I'll try, Mom. Believe me, I'll try."

I BUY A STRAWBERRY MILKSHAKE a few minutes before nine because I don't want Noe to ask me why I'm so far from my old place, but it turns out I don't need a dairy-based cover story because as soon as I get in the car, he launches into an account of his family vacation. Apparently, he met up with his uncle's family in Vegas and had the time of his life.

"My cousin Kiana, the fat one, had this white friend with blue eyes and blonde hair and shit—not fat—and she let me do all kinds of stuff to her."

I tune him out as he lists things, things I don't want to do to girls. Thankfully he moves on to another topic, then another, then another. I only speak up when the rap and reggaeton he's been playing takes a sudden turn.

"Is this Ethel Cain?"

He clears his throat and flicks his nose with his thumb, obviously embarrassed. "Kiana's friend showed it to me. It isn't bad, ya know?"

Moments like these give me hope for Noe. I know the bar is in hell, but my part of town isn't exactly crawling with people who'll put up with me, with my long stretches of silence, with my pessimism, with the walls I don't let down for anyone.

"Yeah," I say. "It's not bad."

"Anyway, you can't say shit with your nails lookin' like that."

"First of all, I *didn't* say anything—I just agreed with you—and second, at least I'm not wearing eyeliner."

The conversation takes a turn that I don't pay too much attention to. Mostly, I'm thinking about what I said, how I was willing to throw someone else under the bus just so I could be safe. It's another reminder that everyone will disappoint you eventually, even yourself.

THE PARTY'S A RAGER BECAUSE, as Noe told me in the car, the guy who's throwing it lives with his cousins, and they "don't give a shit about nothing."

In the kitchen, I pour Jose Cuervo into my and Noe's cups. There's Patrón on the counter, but I assume we're not special enough to drink it. Noe always says he can't taste the difference anyway, which makes me concerned for his taste buds.

We chug our shots, and I pour more Jose. This time, Noe adds some Squirt so we have drinks to walk around the party with. As we do a lap, I try not to walk too close to him—he's said before that "It's hard to spit game when you're so far up my ass you should at least be using Vaseline"—but I also try not to drift away because he's also scolded me for not being a good wingman.

When we reach a mixed gender group of kids from our school, we stop and stand awkwardly next to them as they have a conversation. Eventually the circle opens up when a girl I know from U.S. history class last year notices me and says, "Oh, hey, Adam!"

"Hey, Anna," I say. "This is my friend Noe."

"Nice to meet you," she says.

"You too," he says, his eyes on her tits.

"Oh my God." Anna grabs my hand and holds it up to her face. "Your nails are so cool. Did you do them yourself?"

Okay, I have to think quickly here. What is the least cringey answer to this question? If I painted them myself and did this great a job (because let's face it, they're flawless) then I must have done it many times before, which is suspicious. If someone else painted them, then I'd either have to say it was my mom, which I think would probably sound really weird, or I'd have to say it was Noe, which I'm pretty sure would make him cuss me out right here, right now. So I guess I only have one option.

"Yeah, I did."

"Oh my God!" Anna says again. "That's so impressive. I *love* guys who rock nail polish."

"I was just telling him to do mine," Noe says, getting closer to Anna, "but he's always too busy."

"Oh yeah?" she says. "What's been keeping you busy, Adam?"

You want the real answer? I want to say. *Packing, moving, unpacking, and trying not to think about the fact that my dad would rather I be dead than gay. It's been a real fun, busy time.*

"Not much," is what I actually say.

"You haven't been drawing?" Anna asks. "You were always doing that in history. Some of your stuff was really cool."

"I keep telling him to draw me something I can get tatted," Noe says. "Either here." He lifts up his arm and points to his right bicep. "Or here." He lifts his shirt and pats the lower right side of his flat stomach, the area where I'd cut into if he had appendicitis and I was a surgeon like my mom wants me to be.

Anna drops my hand. "I *love* guys with tattoos."

At least I know exactly what I'm supposed to do now.

After I disappear from the circle, I materialize back in the kitchen. I finish my drink before I take a shot of tequila and head to the backyard. A quick look around reveals I'm the only one here, probably because it's hot as balls.

"I was starting to think no one would ever come out and join me."

I turn to face the voice. Apparently, my quick look around was too quick. There's a guy sitting at a glass table with an umbrella sticking out of it.

"There's a lot going on inside," I say.

"There's a lot going on out here."

I don't reply, and the silence is filled with the sound of crickets. I give him a look.

"Okay, fine," he says. "Nothing's happening *currently*."

"Were you planning on putting on a show?"

Oh, I'm *drunk*. This is further confirmed when I wobble over to the table and take the seat next to him.

"What kind of show?" he asks.

"Cirque du Soleil," I say.

"What does that mean? I failed French."

I snort. He's cute, this guy. Personality wise and otherwise. He's got curly hair, glasses, and a prominent nose.

"Roughly translated, it means backyard moonlit strip show."

He lets out a laugh, and it's big and ragged and makes me want to reach under his shirt and touch the exact spot where it originated.

"Diaphragm," I say softly to myself.

"What?" he says, one of his eyebrows shooting up.

"Diaphragm," I say more firmly.

"Is that a code?"

"Sure."

"Can I get a little more context?"

"No."

"Okay. Well…" He leans in, places his hand on mine (which is on my thigh), and strokes my fingernails. "Is that the answer?"

I should be surprised by his forwardness, by the fact that he knew what I was, *who* I was, but it's so obvious when someone's different, isn't it? It's so obvious when they look at you with a special kind of attentiveness. It's so obvious when someone is going to change your life.

"Close enough," I say before I lean in and kiss him.

I DON'T KNOW HOW LONG my first kiss lasts—whether it's a few seconds or minutes—before Noe bursts into the backyard, sees us, and says, "You gotta be fucking kidding me, bro."

I jump up. "Oh, shit."

"You're fucking joking, right? Like, this gotta be a prank."

For a moment, I consider going with his explanation. *Haha, gotcha, bro. I saw you heading out back, and I thought wouldn't it be fucking hilarious to make you think I like dudes? This guy was in on it because I bet him ten bucks you'd piss yourself.*

But what's the fucking point? I'd only buy myself some time before he caught me doing something else.

"Are you gonna fucking say something?" Noe says.

"Nothing that'll make anything better," I reply.

"Pinche maricón." He shakes his head in disgust and goes back inside.

I guess it could have gone worse. He could have hit me. Or the guy I kissed could have tried to defend me, which would have made me feel guilty that he was fighting my fight.

"I'm sorry," he says.

I ignore his apology and, like I usually do, move on immediately to my next thought. "Huh. I just realized I don't even know your name."

"Oh, it's—"

"Don't tell me." His eyebrows knit together. He's cute when he's confused, which makes saying what I say next hard. "It doesn't matter. I'm gonna go."

"But—"

I take off before he can say anything else.

It takes me two hours to walk home. Noe blows up my phone the whole time. Not to see if I'm okay or offer a ride, obviously.

I never want to see you again.

I can't believe I was friends with someone like you.

Your fucking sick man.

I bet you just wanted me to fuck you.

Fucking sick.

I only reply once.

**you're*

By the time I open the front door, my feet are aching, my back is drenched in sweat, and my throat is scratchy. At least the dehydration means my eyes are dry.

The living room is dark. I can hear my mom's snoring, so I try to walk quietly to my bedroom. Seconds later, however, my pinkie toe catches the leg of the coffee table, and I can't help letting out a string of muttered cuss words.

The lamp beside the couch turns on, and I see my mom's sleepy but concerned face.

"You okay?" she asks.

Even though I'm ninety-nine percent sure she's asking about my toe, I can't help but think she's asking me something else, and for that reason, I can't keep it all in.

I shake my head and sink to the floor, tears finally flooding my eyes. She meets me there, wrapping me in her arms.

As I sob, I think back to when it all started. Maybe if I can pinpoint the moment I became this person, I can undo it. Maybe I can keep everyone who's abandoned me because of what I am.

WHEN I WAS YOUNG, DAD worked during the day and Mom took care of me. She'd make me breakfast and we'd watch Disney movies and sometimes we'd play dress up.

It started off with her modeling her clothes for me, asking me what I liked, stuff like that. But one day I probably stepped into her high heels, and she probably laughed, and I probably loved the sound so much I kept doing it. At one point, I started wearing her purses and her necklaces, not because it amused her but because I wanted to. I didn't feel like putting on makeup or her dresses, but I liked all her accessories. She only had one rule: it all had to come off before Dad came home.

Things changed with nail polish. This, I remember vividly.

I was in the kitchen trying to find the bag of Hot Cheetos that I'd later find out Dad had eaten when the smell of nail polish remover invaded my nostrils. I followed the harsh yet alluring scent to the living room, where I found Mom on the carpet in front of the TV, her fingers splayed as she used cotton balls to rub off purple polish.

When Mom tells the story, she says I walked over to her like a robot and picked up the bottle like I was gonna chug it. But I didn't, obviously. I just wanted to smell it.

"Ay, mijo," she said, grabbing the bottle from me. "That's not good for you."

"You smell permanent markers," I replied.

She was quiet for a bit—a doe in the headlights that could send the car to its room if she wanted to—before she said, "Do as I say—"

"Not as I do," I finished.

"Maybe you should keep smelling this. You're too smart for your age."

"I thought being smart was good."

"Most of the time, but you have to know when to stay quiet."

Anyway, after that exchange, I tried painting her nails, and of course I got polish on her skin and her nail beds and the paper towels protecting the carpet, but she let me keep trying, day after day. Eventually, I wanted polish on my nails, and that's when Mom had an idea. She began putting a topcoat on me, and because it was clear and because Dad didn't pay attention to my tiny, little fingernails at the time, he didn't notice. At least, not for a while.

When he did find out, he didn't blame me. He blamed Mom. After they argued for a long, long time, I told her I didn't want her to paint my nails anymore, and even though she knew I was lying, she stopped. For both our sakes.

I didn't start painting my own nails until high school. Mom was working by then, so I was alone in the house during the summer. In the morning, I'd choose a color from Mom's collection and paint. Horribly, at first. Then, in the late afternoon, I'd remove it before Dad got home. I almost got caught a few times, barely making it to the bathroom with a bottle of nail polish remover before he'd gotten the front door open.

I was officially found out by Mom. Though looking back, she probably knew as soon as her nail polish bottles started running out at an impossible rate. She wasn't mad. She looked at my nails, mouth shrugged, and said, "You need to start doing mine."

That became our bonding ritual. I'd paint her nails at night, in front of the TV, with Dad right beside us. He side-eyed us, but he didn't say anything, which is why after a while I felt safe.

Stupid. So, so stupid.

I STOP CRYING EVENTUALLY. I tell Mom everything that happened, and she says, "I'm sorry" over and over as she rocks me on the living room floor.

I ask her if we can talk about it more in the morning. She says yes, and I trudge down the hallway to the bathroom to brush my teeth. I stare at the mirror, at my hand holding the toothbrush, at my black nails, and fight the urge to gag. I want to strip the polish off, vow to never give myself another manicure again, but I know the drill by now. I'm more than acquainted with my shame. I know it will fade. Tomorrow I'll feel different.

I hope.

I don't turn the light on in my room. I creep forward, my hand in front of me, until I feel my nightstand. My fingers move across the paint swatches on it before I finally find my mattress. As I lie in bed, watching the ceiling fan do lazy circles in the soft light of the liquor store right outside, I can't help but think about the last night me and Mom spent in our old place.

A typical night in front of the TV. Then a "Dad, I have something to tell you…" Then the screaming. And the hitting. And Mom hitting him. And the neighbors getting involved. Mostly I remember the spilled bottles of nail polish.

Before that night, when Dad would go to the bathroom, Mom and I would give the polishes fake names that made us laugh. I'd call her favorite shade of hot pink "slutberry," and she'd pick up a bottle of blue and proclaim it "Smurf phlegm." Dad would walk into the living room and ask what we were giggling about, and we'd say, "Nothing. Just something dumb," and he'd let it go.

I close my eyes and roll over to my side. I guess my life could have been worse. Both my parents could have hated me or been disgusted by me. But at least I have Mom. And the comfort of that thought is enough to allow me to slowly drift to sleep.

I WAKE UP TO THE smell of waffles. I walk robot-like to the kitchen and find Mom at the stove.

"Here you go," she says, turning around with one on a plate.

"Thanks."

I take it from her and walk over to the kitchen table. I grab a knife and fill every square with butter. Then I drown it in syrup and eat. She joins me at some point. We don't talk. We just chew. And swallow. Chew. Swallow.

"Mom," I say when she gets up to put the plates in the sink.

"Yes, mijo?"

"I think I know what color I want to paint my room."

She smiles. "You do?"

I smile back. "Yeah, I do."

SELECTED POEMS BY AARON H. ACEVES

i'm young

i'm young

and i'm sad

and i'm depressed

and i'm unhappy

and i'm dejected

and i'm also horny

and i'm hungry

and i'm a grown-up

and i'm a kid

and i'm "not listening"

and i'm not saying things i want to say

and i'm crying

and i'm laughing

and i'm masturbating

and i'm hating myself

and i'm looking at other people

and i'm wishing i were anyone else

and i'm making my dad angry

and i'm making my mom worry

and i'm telling myself things will get better

and i'm hearing people say, "these are the best years of your life!"

and i'm hoping they're wrong

and i'm hoping i'm right

and i'm fighting the current

and i'm going along

and i'm hoping one day i won't think of her when i hear this song

and i'm dying on the inside

and i'm smiling on the out

and i'm wondering why my words are so low when my thoughts are so loud

and i'm scattered

and i'm scared

and i'm losing my faith

and i'm hearing people say, "*this* is just a phase!"

and i'm reaching

and i'm falling

and i'm ducking

and i'm hearing his voice and all i can think about is… running

and i'm fast with a joke

and i'm slow with a comeback

and i'm looking at them

and i'm saying, "i can't believe you just said that!"

and i'm questioning God because he's not answering my prayers

and i'm seeing them try to take my pride when it's already theirs

and i'm singing off-key

and i'm taking a drink

and i'm driving a car

and i'm not stopping to think

and i'm so so empty

and i'm wondering how that can be when sometimes i feel like i'm filled
to the brink.

chemistry

i hope it isn't only me
who feels the chemistry
the atoms in my body
rearranging
trying
desperately
to get closer to you

You Are

You are the cup from which I cannot drink,
The iceberg that causes my ship to sink.

You are the flame that I must touch,
The vomit I heave when I've drunk too much.

You are a book with a shitty ending,
The one I miss when I stop pretending.

You are a movie that goes on too long,
My confident answer that turns out to be wrong.

You are a song that ends too soon,
I am a werewolf to your full moon.

You are the light of the squad car before I'm arrested,
The trial I face when I don't want to be tested.

You are the acceptance I've had to seek,
Not a vision of heaven, just…a peek.

WHILE YOU WERE SLEEPING: CHAPTER 4

Elisa Park

SeoHee Yoon -
17 Years Old

PURPLE LIGHTS HUNG FROM EVERY corner of my bedroom, complementing the moonlight that shone in from the window. My photo wall of polaroids hung above my desk to remind me of my happy memories. My boba tea plushie squished underneath my chest as I laid on my stomach with the blanket over me and my AirPods playing "Heaven" by BTOB. Being unable to sleep in the middle of the night used to scare me, but nowadays I felt less scared and more relaxed knowing I wasn't alone.

Sleep never came when I waited, but YoHan did.

I miss you.

I sent the text on a random night at a random time knowing he would reply. He always did. Late into the night and everyone was fast asleep except us. We were wide awake with eyes open at our screens, waiting for the next text to bloom.

YoHan asked me what I was doing. I answered in the same way I'd always done: thinking of you. He offered a smiley face emoji, asking what else I'd done. I recalled my day, specifying how I drank enough water, cooked my meals, took my meds, and did my skincare routine with a new mask pack. But then I texted how tired I was. It was the kind of tiredness that was so bone deep it never went away. There was no cure. Except YoHan. If I was his vitamin, then he was my medicine. I didn't say that. YoHan did. He made me smile and asked me to smile tomorrow too.

YoHan needed to go to sleep as I did for school tomorrow. But I was scared, scared that he'd leave for good. I didn't want him to leave. But YoHan reminded me that we had tomorrow. He promised to text me tomorrow too. Even when he was with me at that moment, I missed him.

I'm right here, he said.

I know.

I have a surprise for you tomorrow.

What is it?

You'll find out if you fall asleep. Let's meet in our dreams.

YoHan asked to meet me in my dreams. I agreed. But sometimes these moments felt like nothing but a dream. And once I woke up in the morning, it would have all been a dream.

I didn't want to fall into his dreams again…

In a gentle whisper, he wished me sweet dreams.

I dozed off thanks to his audio message because he helped me fall asleep better than any amount of Valium ever could.

"Noona, wake up! We can't be late for school!" JaeYoon yelled from the bathroom that connected both of our rooms. His Bluetooth speaker was already blasting that one viral song from TikTok on loop as he turned the shower on.

I trudged into the bathroom with my fluffy lilac slippers, squinting at the bright white lights. Umma had stuck another pink Post-it note to the side mirror, adding it to her Post-it heart wall of Bible verses. But instead of a Bible verse, it had a message on it: Happy Birthday to my lovely daughter, SeoHee.

Today was my seventeenth birthday.

I brushed through my hair that had grown all the way past my ribcage; it used to barely touch my collarbone. I once contemplated killing myself in the bathtub by submerging myself or slitting a vein, but I didn't want Umma, Appa, or JaeYoon to discover my corpse like that. That's why I went to the beach in the middle of the night when everyone slept so that my body would float away into the ocean far away. I refrained from cutting it since I left the hospital. I wanted it to serve as a reminder of how much time has passed and how I was grateful to be breathing today.

I glanced at my reflection in the mirror and reminded myself of my goal: let's get through the day.

After finishing sixth period AP U.S. History, I waited in the parking lot for JaeYoon to finish swim practice with the water polo team. When I first transferred to Chadwick, I stuck out like a sore thumb with my decade-old pre-owned Lexus in the sea of Teslas, BMWs, and Maseratis.

But now, I appreciated how easy it was for me to find my car in the student parking lot.

Once JaeYoon arrived, he threw his duffle bag and backpack into the back seat and immediately disconnected my Spotify for his. I let him play his song as I backed out of the parking space and toward the intersection to leave campus.

JaeYoon kept switching songs before they even finished, annoying me. I turned the volume down only for him to raise it. He also wasn't letting me listen to my songs. We had an agreement to take turns playing our playlist. I needed music to stay awake or else I would zone out because of how sleep-deprived I was. But last night, I slept okay.

"Noona!" JaeYoon practically ripped my arm from the tendon the way he yanked it so hard. Shaking him off, I pressed on the gas to go straight when a black Porsche SUV headed toward us instead of stopping at the light.

I immediately braked, throwing my right arm across JaeYoon's chest.

The collapsing of metal screeched.

My neck whipped forward as my car wouldn't stop beeping. My heart fell to my stomach. This could have turned out way worse if I accidentally pressed the gas instead of the brake. Thank goodness, I didn't.

I turned to the side to check JaeYoon, but he had already left the vehicle. A crowd of students began to form near us. I immediately got out to see who the other driver was. It was none other than one of the entitled Chadwick moms with perfectly blown out hair and a Chanel bag who deluded themselves into thinking they owned the school because of their hefty semester donations. But I was ready to stand up to her because she was the one who was in the wrong, not me. Why would she run a stop sign in the middle of a school zone where students and kids from the equestrian club were walking about?

"Are you kids okay? The school zone monitor ran over to us, waving their bright red LED stick.

"I'm never getting in the car when you're driving again!" JaeYoon kicked the fragment of the shattered car's side-view mirror towards the curb, which I rushed to take a photo of along with the rest of the damage to my car.

"You kids go to the nurse's office, I'll handle things here." The school zone monitor ushered us toward another teacher who stood by the gate on patrol.

"YOU'RE NOT HURT, RIGHT?" I asked JaeYoon as the nurse inspected him. He appeared perfectly fine sitting on the stool except for his mouth that wouldn't stop yapping about how I was to blame for this.

"Get some rest and lay down on the beds while I notify your parents." The nurse left to call my mom, leaving me alone in the office. Meanwhile, JaeYoon stomped off because he was righteously pissed off at me.

I sat on one of the beds and closed the curtains, holding myself to self-soothe. The nurse's office had the AC on full blast and reeked of disinfectant. It reminded me of the hospital ward I used to stay in and I despised it. I tapped in my AirPods, listening to my playlist to help calm myself down as if I could get rid of all the blame I felt for almost endangering my little brother's life and ruining the car my parents gifted me last year.

I noticed a pair of gray Dior B27s approaching me. YoHan. He swept open the curtains by my bed and I took out my AirPods. YoHan crouched by my bed and held my hands.

"The driver should have stopped but she didn't—"

I caught a glimpse of his shadow. I hadn't seen it in a very long time. I prayed it would lose to the sun, but it didn't. He didn't try to hide it. His eyes never swayed from mine, bleary and red from restless nights. He broke the silence, his voice dropping an octave lower and thick with pure sadness.

"It was you who ran the red light."

I counted back, checking how many hours I'd slept last night. I went to sleep a bit past midnight after listening to YoHan's audio message and woke up twice, but I slept at least six hours? Didn't I? I couldn't remember. I couldn't focus.

"I did…?" I didn't want to believe it.

The split in him cracked. YoHan crushed me in his embrace, bawling onto my shoulder like he was heaving his guts out. His chest quivered against me. Worried he was barely breathing, I strained to make some space between us. YoHan looked at me as if I ripped off his Band-Aid without a warning.

I looked around for a tissue near the beds but couldn't find one. Given how exorbitant their tuition was, I grew frustrated by the lack of accessible tissues. I lifted the sleeve of my shirt to soak his tears, but he cried right through them. Shades of red and pink tinged the skin around his eyes. In the reflection of his tears, I saw mine were too.

He hugged me so close our bones touched. The strands of YoHan's bleached hair tickled my neck along with his warm breaths. I remembered his hair used to be longer because he couldn't get a haircut while hospitalized. His hair used to be the color of sunshine. But now YoHan's hair was the color of moonlight.

As I ran my fingers through its surprisingly soft strands, hints of his natural black hair peeked through. The boy who was his mom's sunshine came to resent the sun. Others healed, yet his mom didn't. Others lived, yet his mom didn't. His eyes no longer gleamed with joy. Only crescent shadows clung underneath his eyes. He was no longer the sunshine his mom loved.

"I'm glad you're alive," YoHan whispered.

I was too. At least I was alive…but I couldn't help but think: When would I be better?

SHINY ROSE GOLD BALLOONS DECORATED the vanilla cream wall, spelling out "Happy 17th Birthday" with pink heart balloons taped around it. The dining table sat in front of it, making it the perfect photo spot. Wearing the rose gold tiara Umma bought me for last year's birthday and a pink birthday sash over my ivory lace dress, I smiled as Umma took photos to send to our relatives in Seoul. I handed JaeYoon my phone and Polaroid to take photos of me holding the lilac cake YoHan gifted me. I didn't expect his surprise to be a whole birthday cake he decorated exactly like the aesthetic lunchbox cakes I'd been saving to my Pinterest boards. JaeYoon rolled his eyes as I smiled for the photos. The corners of my lips wilted at his scowl. He was upset that our parents didn't scold me for the car accident.

Sitting down at the table, Appa led the dinner prayer and gestured for us to join hands. I grabbed Umma and JaeYoon's as Appa thanked the Lord for our dinner and the fact that JaeYoon and I didn't suffer any more serious injury in the crash.

"우리 소중한 딸 서희가 우리 곁에 있어서 주님한테 감사를 표현합니다. 아멘." (I express gratitude to the Lord for our precious daughter SeoHee being by our side. Amen.)

"Amen." Before I let go of their hands, I couldn't help but constantly feel bad about what happened today. It was all my fault, but my insomnia wasn't exactly something I could control…

Dismissing the thoughts, I disassembled the beautiful pot of mille-feuille nabe in the center of the dining table onto my plate.

"Gosh, this is so good," JaeYoon moaned, as we fought over the last piece with our metal chopsticks.

"Then you should learn how to make it instead of asking me and Umma to cook for you all the time."

"You think I ask because I don't know how?"

"Says the dude who doesn't even know where the kitchen knives are. Then why do you ask me to cook for you all the time?"

"Cause you don't eat unless I ask you to cook for me."

I always thought my little brother was annoying me by asking me to make him food. I didn't know that it was his unique way of looking after me. My Valium and Zoloft prescriptions killed my appetite, but I made the effort to eat by meal prepping our lunches for school.

"윤재윤." Umma called JaeYoon by his full Korean name, which got him to stop because it meant our parents meant business.

JaeYoon let go of the last piece of beef and took a spoonful of the seaweed soup instead. I took the last piece and finished my bowl.

I reached for my glass of water to swallow the four colorful pills that always reminded me of Skittles. I washed it down with a huge bite of the dark chocolate cake.

I LOOKED UP FROM MY phone when someone violently knocked on my door. It was JaeYoon. He threw a small perfectly wrapped box into my palms along with an envelope. It was too neat for him to have wrapped. He must have asked Umma to wrap it for him. I ripped open the wrapping paper to unveil a box of Polaroid film.

"Let's celebrate next year too." JaeYoon said, crossing the hall into his bedroom, forgetting for the billionth time to close the door on his way out.

"Thanks!" I shouted after him only to hear his door slamming shut.

I grabbed the envelope and turned it to the front. It wasn't a birthday card from JaeYoon, but a letter addressed to me from me. When did I write this? The letter was dated three years ago.

The meaning behind JaeYoon's words settled like a pill dissolving inside my stomach. Another birthday meant another year alive.

I was seventeen years old now, which meant that I'd been breathing for a total of seventeen years.

For seventeen years I'd constantly been surprised to wake up every morning to experience a new day. Because I never once believed I would live to see my sixteenth birthday. I never once believed I would end up attending my junior year at the elite private school that was Chadwick. I never once believed I would live past sixteen. I never once believed I would meet someone like YoHan. I never once believed I would have the will and courage to continue breathing.

Three years had passed, meaning three birthdays had passed. Three years of school had passed. Three years had passed since the day I was given a second chance at life.

I ripped open the envelope and pulled the heavily creased paper out.

To 17-year-old SeoHee.

From 14-year-old SeoHee.

A silent gasp left my lips as I recalled the envelope. One day before I left the hospital Dr. Ji wanted me to write a reflection, so I opted to write a letter to my future self.

I had always been terrified of regressing back to my fourteen-year-old self, who was filled with nothing but self-loathing, insecurity, and pain. Every day, the manhole inside me only grew bigger and bigger.

Over the three years I had changed drastically for the better. I was now proud of the life I lived and who I was as a person. I sliced across the sealed envelope with my decorative knife and took out the heavily creased paper.

Dear 17-year-old SeoHee,

Congrats, you made it. You made it to seventeen. Congratulations! The reason why you're reading this letter is because you're breathing right now and I want to remind you how big of an accomplishment that is. Even if all you did was breathe today, I'm proud of you. It is your existence that matters and that no matter how draining today was, tomorrow is another day. You've been granted a tomorrow and never take that for granted. Never.

Place your hand over your heart. Feel that beating? Your heart is beating for a purpose and that purpose is happiness. What's the point of life without happiness? Don't let your self-loathing steal that from you again. Right now, you're happy and you've learned to love yourself the way YoHan loves you. You've learned that Safiya wasn't a good friend to you and that you shouldn't feel guilty for ending the friendship. Friends shouldn't make you feel inferior and hate yourself.

I hope you're so happy that you go to bed every day with a proud smile on your face. Your pillows are dry every morning and you're excited for the day ahead. If today is not that day, then tomorrow will be. Remember that. Tomorrow will be a better day. Good luck and I hope you are able to have happy days.

P.S. I wonder if seventeen-year-old SeoHee will still love YoHan or will she have forgotten him? I hope not. Even if you can't see him, live happily while thinking of him.

From your fourteen-year-old self.

Sincerely,

SeoHee.

My vision blurred. *Tomorrow is another day*. I had tomorrow. Who would have known that I would live to see this day or to read this letter? I surely didn't. With every soft breath I took I felt the strong beating of my heart through my chest and my pulse. My veins throbbed as I held onto the sheet of paper.

It's okay to not be okay. It's okay to cry. But it wasn't okay to give up and I wouldn't.

Teardrops landed on the letter as my face scrunched up in sobs. Raking my fingers through my hair, I steadied my breathing.

I was becoming a better version of myself. When I left, I had this vision of who I wanted to be. I wanted to be someone that was honest, strong, confident, and thriving to be the best version of herself. Becoming this version hadn't been easy or smooth at all. It wasn't always smiles and laughter, but weary smiles and exhausting days. But in the end, I survived it all and was closer to the version I imagined.

I didn't submit to my impulse and self-harm. No. I allowed myself to cry it out. Because everything would be alright. Setting the letter down, I lowered my face into a Kleenex tissue.

Exhaling, I smiled at my reflection in the mirror of the vanity I'd decorated with polaroids of my happy memories.

Everything will be okay. If not today, then tomorrow.

I stuck the letter into my Burn Diary, as I liked to call it, and ran down the stairs toward the fireplace.

LEAFING THROUGH MY JOURNAL, I ripped out today's entry where I word vomited about my insomnia and how it almost cost me my life and JaeYoon's. I was supposed to be his older sister and yet I put him in danger because of my insomnia. I was solely to blame.

Whenever I had bad thoughts, I word vomited onto the page and then burned them to forget about them for good. I threw the inked pages into the fire and watched the flames engulf them. It was refreshing, like the breeze after being confined in a stuffy hospital room.

My phone lit up with a text exactly one minute before midnight. It was none other than YoHan.

Audio Message: "Happy Birthday to SeoHee. Did you like my surprise? I spent two days baking and decorating it. I'm so glad you enjoyed the cake. Let's continue making more precious and beautiful memories together like today. Remember I'm just a supporting character in your story. You're the main character. Sweet dreams, SeoHee. I always hope you'll sleep well. See you tomorrow. Mhwa~"

I snapped a picture of the Polaroid selfie I took with YoHan today in the nurse's office and texted it to him as my reply. The flash whitewashed us terribly like ghosts, but we still smiled despite being drained from all the crying. The tears in our eyes appeared like diamonds clinging to our tear ducts. YoHan was such an endearing crybaby.

A thin trail of smoke stung my nose, but I didn't mind it one bit. My dad suggested I use his old paper shredder to throw away my diary entries, but I wanted the cathartic release of watching something burn. The mechanical whirring of a paper shedding couldn't compare to the dramatic flare of burning paper. Luckily, Dad agreed—as long as I kept the fireplace tidy after every burn.

I replayed the audio message with my AirPods as the scary memory of today's car accident and the diary entry diminished into nothing but soot.

Burn the bad memories; collect the happy ones.

I clasped my hands together as the last ember flickered. My birthday wish was for all those who attempted suicide to be given a second chance to live.

Just like me and Yohan.

ABOUT THE BOY

Leah Nicole Whitcomb

Holding a cup of rooibos tea, I stand on the porch. The cicadas hum while I wait for Kamron. This is the only way that I can avoid talking to Mom. Since Tuesday, I've been hiding out in my room after school, only coming out to grab dinner and then rushing back. Kamron pulls up five minutes till five. When he parks, he pops a mint in his mouth before flinging his bookbag over his shoulder and walking towards me. I offer a tight-lipped smile and a wave, but his smile widens enough for his teeth to graze his lips. I clear my throat to loosen the sudden tightness.

"Didn't get lost again, did you?"

Oh my god, Naima. Is that the best you can come up with? This is like his fourth time coming over. I forcibly blink away the embarrassment, but he chuckles.

"Nah. I'm getting pretty good at finding the place. Didn't even have to use GPS this time."

"That's good," I say, opening the door for him to pass by.

We sit at the kitchen table, and Mom's standing at the bar. While Kamron pulls out his laptop and plugs it in, she asks if we need any drinks or snacks. I lift my mug and avert my gaze. I don't want her thinking I want to talk to her anytime soon. Kamron tells her that he's fine, and she leaves us alone.

"This may be wildly inappropriate, but it feels like you and your mom—" Kamron says. "Yeah," I gnaw my inner lip. "She's never happy when I get in trouble at school."

"I'm sorry about that."

"This is actually not your fault." Unlike the first time when he, Dustin, and Mrs. Truss were definitely to blame. This time was also Mrs. Truss's fault, but apparently teachers are faultless angels who never do anything wrong. "Do you want me to talk to her?"

"No," I scoff.

"Moms love me." He smiles, and I wonder if Moms feel the same way about his smile as I do.

"I don't know how you talking to her is gonna help."

"How about this?" he clears his throat and then loudly says, "Wow, Naima you're so smart. I'm so lucky to have you as my lab partner. I'd completely fail this class if it wasn't for you."

I cover my mouth to muffle my laughter.

"Was that good?" he whispers. "Maybe I could add. 'She's certainly not a delinquent.'" I giggle. "I think that's enough. She's gonna think I put you up to it."

"Okay, then I'll say: 'She did not put me up to this.'"

"Yeah," I nod. "That's really good. Very convincing."

My mouth spreads into an unbelievably wide grin and so does his. When I realize that I may have been staring at him for too long, I grab my mug and bring it up to my lips. Once I sip the tea, I ask about the lab report.

He opens the laptop and pulls up the Google Doc. "I saw you filled out most of the lab report. I'm not kidding. You make me feel like I'm not pulling my weight."

"I had free time this weekend, so I figured I'd just work on it." I shrug. "I finished the lab report. You can, um, read over it. If you want."

He lowers the brightness of the screen and turns the computer towards me. I read over it and notice how he cleaned up my text, fixing my typos and run-ons, but also how clean his copy is.

"Looks good," I tell him when I finish reading. "And we just copy and paste that into a PowerPoint?"

"Pretty much."

We make slides out of each section. There are a few sections for the experiments and the data. After debating between hyperrealistic photos and clip art, we decide to use clip art for the pictures. We read over each slide again, checking for typos and double-checking to make sure the information is correct. When it's to our liking, we decide that we'll alternate slides when it's time to present. Kamron emails the PowerPoint to Mrs. Truss, CCs me, and closes his laptop. We've officially finished our first outside lab.

"Is it cool if I hang out here?" Kamron asks.

It takes me a while to answer because I'm surprised by his request. He usually leaves when we're done, but I guess now that we're "friends," we can hang out. Markese is yelling and playing *Fall Guys* with his door open upstairs.

"Yeah. Do you want to go outside?"

He agrees, so I grab a throw blanket from the couch and follow him out the back door. The buzzing cicadas greet us as we walk on the back porch. The setting sun casts shades of orange, pink, and yellow on the horizon. We sit on the porch swing on the side of the house, and I look out to the corn stalks. The humid air drapes us.

"I've been thinking about what you and Luna said," Kamron starts, "About going to Homecoming?"

"Yeah. Are you going?" I wrap the blanket around me.

"Kennedy asked me, but I told her no." He rubs his palms together. "I don't know if I want to be friends with her. Especially after how she treated you."

"Oh." I chew my inner lip. "I don't—you don't have to do that for me."

"Yeah, I know, but I want to." His smile is closed, showing a hint of a dimple. How does he have such a perfect face? "Were you two close?"

I nod. "Before Luna moved here, it used to be me, her, Sam, and my other cousin, Eric. And every summer we used to play together out there." I point backwards to the patch of land between mine and Sam's house. "We even went to a Little Mix concert together."

"Oh, that band you claimed is better than Beyoncé?"

"I didn't say better than Beyoncé," I clarify. "I said better than Destiny's Child. There's a difference."

He squints to hint that he doesn't believe me.

"But anyway," I smile, remembering the story, "I heard Little Mix was coming to New Orleans. It was the first—and now I realize only— tour they did in the US, and I *begged* my dad to take me. Kennedy was a *huge* Ariana Grande fan—she probably still is—and Little Mix was opening for her. And she also begged Dad to take us, and he did, even though it was a school night. When we got there, I was under the same roof as Little Mix, and it was like I was complete. Like I've heard every single song they sang and can tell their voices apart and here I am seeing the real life people behind the voice. It. Was. Magical."

I shake my head and smile. I live streamed their last show a couple of years ago. Seeing these women who had been such an instrumental part of my life filled my heart with joy. And even though they're broken up or "on hiatus," I'm so glad I got to be part of their journey.

"Like I'm so glad they exist, and I got to experience them," I tell him.

I turn over to look at Kamron, and he's just staring at me. I probably lost him a while ago, so I clear my throat and get back on topic.

"Um, the concert was good and once Ariana Grande came on, the noise was too loud and the lights were too bright so I had to tap out, and Dad had made friends with these college students there. I think they were like the only adults in our section. Their names were—" I close my eyes to try and remember it. "Catherine and Leah. And they were really nice and Leah offered to sit outside with me because my head was banging and when we got back to school, all Kennedy talked about was seeing Ariana Grande, and I felt bad because I missed most of her set." I sigh. "I'm sorry. That's my favorite memory, but it's also kinda sad."

"No, I'm glad you felt comfortable enough to share that with me. I'm honored." He places his hands over his heart and smiles.

I pull the blanket tighter around my arms and rock.

"I wanted to ask you about your garden." Kamron points to the backyard. "I see it every time I come over. And I was just wondering… do you really grow food?"

I snicker at his silly question. "Yeah. I grow food." "By yourself?"

"Yeah." I nod, shocked that he thinks it's hard. "Come on."

I stand up and wait for him to join me. Turning on my phone's flashlight, we walk down the stairs to the little plot of land I grow food on. In the front are a row of sunflowers to encourage the pollinators to pollinate my food plants. I squat and touch a thick brown vine. "This gave me about five tomatoes before it was done."

"Here," I turn to the row beside it, "I got a bunch of green beans from this. We ate them on Labor Day, actually."

Kamron squats down with me, turning the thin greenish vines over in his hands. I stand up and take a couple more steps. I point to a bunch of purple triangular leaves. "These are my sweet potatoes. They should be ready soon. And this," —I turn my flashlight to the indentation amongst the yellowing leaves on the ground— "is where I grew my watermelon."

"You grew a watermelon?" he asks, eyes wide.

"It was really good." I smile, proud of my work. "And of course, this," —I point to the stalks— "is corn."

His hands run over the stalk, studying the broad green leaves. I see an ear that is pretty done and pull it off. "You can have this if you want?" I offer it to him.

"No, no," he waves his hands, "I don't want to take your corn." "It's just corn. You can try it. Tell me how it tastes."

"Thanks." He grabs it. "So what made you start gardening?"

"Um…my dad." I gulp and clutch the blanket tighter. We walk back towards the porch. "When I was younger and we first moved out here, he wanted a garden so bad. It was a lot bigger than the one I have now. I thought the same as you when the garden grew. Like we put a seed in the ground, and it grew into food? It blew my mind." I laugh, remembering my awe that first summer we had a garden. How Dad had us drag bags of compost and soil to the garden. How hot it was and how much we complained. But also, how much it was worth it when we took our first bite of the food we made.

I nibble my bottom lip. "I guess—I guess I keep the garden going because if it's still here, so is he."

Looking back at my garden that's about a quarter of the size of his, I may not have always liked the work, but it was one of those things that we regularly did together. It was one of the few things that brought us joy.

"I think he'd be proud of you."

My attention turns back to Kamron who stands on the top step. He offers his hand to me to help me up the stairs. I take it and share a small smile. "Thanks."

We return to the porch swing and sit close enough that our thighs touch. I rock the swing remembering the last time I saw Dad. Mom was making a casserole and forgot cheese, the most important part. Dad offered to drive into town. He didn't even say bye to us because he was so sure he'd be back. We were so sure he'd be back.

After an hour, he still wasn't home. Mom was about to get in the car herself and find Dad, when the police called saying he hit a deer, and like that, I didn't have a dad anymore. He was gone. In a year where 350,000 Americans died from a novel virus, my dad died in a car accident. It seemed there was no room to grieve because everyone else had it so much worse.

A tear falls down my face from the memory. I wipe it away and sniffle. "You good?" he asks.

"Sorry." I shake my head. "I'm a mess."

When he gently wipes the tear from my cheek, I touch the damp streak it leaves.

"I don't think you're a mess." He ducks his head to enter my line of sight. When I look at him, he smiles. Goosebumps spread across my chest. "I wasn't trying to overstep—"

"No, it's not that." I shake my head again. "I just thought about the last time I saw my dad. He died in a, um…a car accident. We did all this work, you know, to avoid getting Covid, and he died because of a fucking deer." I bury my face in my hands.

I didn't even get to see him again. Because of social distancing, we couldn't have a funeral or see the body. He was gone. Forever.

Kamron rubs my arm, and it soothes a lot of the dread. I gaze up at the sky, the stars twinkling.

"You know," I sniffle and wipe a tear away, "when I was younger, I used to think we turned into stars when we die. Like it made sense. If Heaven and angels were in the sky, why wouldn't the stars be the people who went to Heaven? I—" I bite my bottom lip. "I hope that Dad is a star. That although he doesn't exist here with us, he still exists in the universe."

"Hmmm," Kamron hums, "kinda like how energy is never created or destroyed?"

"Exactly!" I smile, happy we're on the same page. "Did you know that it takes years for the light from the stars to reach us, so by the time we see it, the star itself could be gone? It's like the star exists and doesn't exist at the same time? And maybe that's how death is. We exist and don't exist at the same time." "Like memories?"

"Yeah, like memories. Like we exist in someone's memory, which is real—an existence—but we also don't. We are not the same as we were in those memories. We evolve and change, but also memories are fallible, so there's that. And the light that we see from the stars are the memories of the stars themselves."

My heart swells as I stare back up at the night sky. This is the first time that someone's given me the space to talk about my dad and death. Anytime I brought it up to Luna or Sam, they froze—like they were tired of me talking about him, but they couldn't say anything to the girl whose parent died. Mom got harder on me, and Markese retreated into video games. It's why I started visiting Dad at his grave. It was the only chance

I got to talk to and about him. Sitting here with Kamron now, I don't feel the raw vulnerability that comes with talking about Dad. Instead, it's a release. I feel understood. Seen.

"Naima?"

He lays his hand on top of mine. I look at it and then back up at him. The distant smell of watermelon Ice Breaker is on his tongue. His face is so close to mine that I can feel his breath on my lips. My eyes travel from his lips to his eyes which are as sure as mine. When his hand reaches around my waist, bringing me closer to him, I do it. I lean over to fill the gap between us and kiss him. My first kiss. His beautiful lips are as soft as I suspected, and he grabs my nape, pulling me closer to him when—

"Nai!"

I jump back and clutch my chest. My heartbeat races as Sam's heavy footsteps come up the stairs and drag across the porch. We stare at each other with faces full of something akin to guilt.

"Nai?"

"I'm back here," I call from the side of the house.

"Nai, I need your help with—oh," Sam says once he sees Kamron.

Kamron turns back to me. "I'm gonna go. Thank you…for the corn." He waves the ear in the air. "Good seeing you again, Sam."

I wave goodbye to Kamron. When the car door shuts, I let the breath I'm holding go. "What's that about?" Sam asks, pointing to Kamron's car.

"Nothing. What's wrong, Sam?" I try to muffle the devastation in my voice.

"You know, Homecoming's in two weeks?" He sits down on the swing and grabs my hands. "I kinda need your help picking a suit."

My eyes widen, and I lightly slap his arm. "Sam, no. How do you not have your suit already?"

"I was waiting on y'all to pick your dresses so we can coordinate. You know how long girls take to get ready." He playfully rolls his eyes.

"I know you're not talking. We always have to wait for you, Mr. Wait-till-the-Last Minute." I grab my phone from my pocket. "Let's hope we can find you a suit before the dance."

When I find a decent site, I give him the phone to look for a suit. While he's scrolling, I touch my lips and remember the warmth of Kamron's kiss.

POLYURETHANE

Mariella Isabel Acevedo

(Polyurethane: any class of synthetic

resinous, fibrous, or elastomeric

compounds. Used mainly in

memory foam.)

scrapping paper after paper

after paper after

paper

we learn the hard way that sometimes pencil cannot be

erased we are fatuous

picking up and putting down the graphite ad libitum

the pen is mightier than the sword and the pencil slices just as
easy

is not until regretful fingers frantically scrub at the evidence of our

touch we consider the delicacy of (im)permanence

we teach ourselves to be light-handed…that is until we learn the lesson

again our bodies like scrapbooks collecting scars, stretch marks, wrinkles

and those that fade

become a twisted case of object permanence when gazing in the

mirror the vessels that broke and bled under the surface of your skin

the kiss of him

and her

and him

and her

there is no residue I can erase away; it is simply ingrained into
me

my body may as well be made of paper

or polyurethane

2013/2019

Joya Breinholt

2013

THE TALL PINE TREES REFLECT in the windows of the rental car. It's been nearly ten minutes since her parents left and went into the house, but Joya made them put down the window as she slid into the front seat so she could fix her hair in the rearview mirror.

It's only the first month of the summer, so she hasn't quite gotten as dark as she will by August, but she wonders how much deeper her skin will be than her cousins. She's painfully aware that her skin will be the factor, more than her different home or religion or parents, that will make her stick out like a sore thumb in the photos they take that summer. She'll have to look at those photos for the next year before she sees her cousins again.

But it's hard to dwell on that when anticipation is building in her stomach, like little butterflies. She has two weeks to give her cousins a new impression to remember her by for the next year, to convince them that she's a sort of different, effortless cool that nobody from her real life sees her as. They all might be a bit too aware of how her skin is darker than theirs, how she doesn't go to the local church with them on Sunday. She can't change those things to fit in. But she can pretend—to be different in a fun, cool way that makes them *want* to be with her.

As she looks in the mirror a final time, she's almost convinced that she looks like who she wants to be. It's going to be a perfect summer.

IT WAS INDEED PERFECT, AT least initially. Joya walks into the vacation home that she knows like the back of her hand, and her two favorite cousins are waiting for her by the window. They shriek and hug, and it's like no time has passed since they saw each other last. Distance and differences are to be forgotten as Ruth chatters about the new Taylor Swift album that they're all obsessed with, and Libby interjects to mention they're getting slushies after they go to the beach, a family tradition.

They find themselves in one of the attic bedrooms, sitting on the blue-and-green bedding that hasn't been switched out in years. They're talking about the plans for the beach and plans for a late dinner when *it* comes up.

Ruth makes an offhand comment about the dinner prayer, and Joya looks down. Two pairs of blue eyes meet Joya's brown ones. After realizing why Joya is so reluctant to speak about the prayer, Libby is the first to speak.

"You *don't* pray?" she says, not quite mean-spiritedly but not quite nicely, either. Joya feels her shoulders tug up to her ears as shame creeps across her cheeks. With them staring at her like she's an alien, she certainly doesn't feel cool or fun or included. She's desperate for anything to say, to distract them. She settles on a memory: her grandmother—her maternal one, not the one she shares with these cousins—in her pooja prayer, kneeling in Hindu prayer.

"I *Indian* pray," she tells them, even though she's never joined her grandmother in prayer. But she hates this feeling of embarrassment building up inside of her, and she's willing to say anything to get them to stop looking at her like that. And even though the feeling of shame doesn't subside for a while, Ruth redirects the conversation, and everything feels better.

BETWEEN THE FIVE FAMILIES AND thirteen cousins, there's rarely a peaceful moment in Lake Tahoe. But they do happen once in a blue moon. Sand Harbor Beach is like an oasis from the noise.

It's hard not to feel at peace while laying on a raft in the middle of the lake with Ruth and Libby. The water in Tahoe is always cold, but the sun shines brightly down on them. It's a comfortable moment of silence, a memory that Joya will hold onto until she returns next year.

The only people out of spirits are Joya's parents. They stretch out their towels on the white sand a bit far from the rest of the aunts and uncles, and while Joya can't hear them, she knows they're complaining that the family went to Sand Harbor instead of the beach with a snack bar. She catches one of her uncles side-eyeing the beer in her dad's hand.

But unlike her parents, she loves Sand Harbor with her whole heart. She's been looking forward to returning here for a year. She thinks she could stay here forever. But soon, Ruth lifts her head at the sound of somebody splashing towards them.

As Jake approaches, Joya knows something is up. Ruth's brother Jake is seven years older than them, and he never gave the three of them a second glance at the beach. Maybe, Joya thinks with a thrill, the three of them are finally older enough to tag along on his adventures.

"You guys want to jump off that rock with us?" Jack asks Ruth, pointing to the largest cliff on the shore. It looks extremely sharp, in Joya's opinion. And very, *very* tall.

Something pierces through Joya's stomach. "No," she says instantly. Ruth and Libby, who had been smiling excitedly before, look at her in horror.

"What do you mean, *'No*?'" Ruth demands.

"Are you kidding?" Joya says, feeling a bit bashful but still very set on *not* jumping. "It's so dangerous! That's, like, a thirty-foot fall. What if there's rocks below and you hit your head?" She can see Jake roll his eyes, but she doesn't care.

Ruth is mad, though. "It's not dangerous at all! We did the same thing in Newport Beach last year, and it was *so* fun."

Joya sets her jaw. "If you want to be *stupid* and jump, that's not my problem. I'll be waiting here." She crosses her arms and turns her back to the three of them. She doesn't really expect Ruth and Libby to go. She figured they'd be smart enough to decide against it, and at the very least, she thought they wouldn't leave her alone. They do go, though, and Joya watches as all her cousins—even the ones younger than her—jump off the cliff, howling in delight and swimming happily in the water below. She doesn't regret not jumping, exactly—there's nothing in the world that could convince her that it's safe. And maybe her cousins, who regularly ski and snowboard and raft because there simply isn't anything else to do in Utah, are comfortable taking physical risks like that, but she sure as hell isn't.

Still, it's hard not to feel bitter watching from the sidelines. She's been looking forward to being here with them all year, but watching them laugh as they jump off the rock, she has never felt so distant.

2019

THE TALL PINE TREES REFLECT in the windows of the rental car. She almost makes her parents put down the window so she can fix her hair in the rearview mirror before she goes in, but before she can speak, she changes her mind.

She remembers how worried she was about being dark six years earlier. With humor and a bit of uneasiness, she thinks that her younger self would be even more horrified today; her coloring has only gotten darker as she's grown up. Skin that once would have passed as white skin that's tanned is now clearly ethnic. She sticks out even more among her white cousins.

She's more confident going in than she was six years ago—she's more put together now, with styled and highlighted hair, a cute outfit, and a greater sense of self from a year of high school—but the anticipatory butterflies in her stomach still persist. A tiny, traitorous part of her still wants it to be perfect. It's been a year since she last saw her cousins, and a part of her wants them to know how great her life in the city on the East Coast is, wants them to think that she's smart and interesting and cultured, so that they still want to be around her despite the differences that have only become more apparent with time.

But the darkness of her skin serves as a reminder: even the things she tried to ignore and perfect show their cracks over time. She knows it's futile to try and act like she's not different, and it's relieving.

She doesn't even try to comb her hair or apply lip gloss before jumping out of the car and running into the house. She knows who she would see if she looked in the mirror: herself, no more and no less. It's going to be a great summer.

Between the five families and thirteen cousins, there's rarely a peaceful moment in Lake Tahoe. But they do happen once in a blue moon.

Joya sits on the stone front steps of the house one afternoon, the sunset glowing orange. A few moments earlier, she'd waved to Libby and Ruth as they biked to the 7-Eleven to get Slurpees for everybody. She's painting her toes a dark green, like the color of the Tahoe pine trees. She hopes that the pedicure will last until she gets back to DC, like a souvenir.

It's so quiet that she's immediately aware when the front door opens behind her. Swiping a final coat on her big toe, she turns away to see Jem, Libby's five-year-old little brother. He has the blue eyes that every Breinholt but Joya has, and he has Libby's blonde hair. If you saw him and Joya on the street, you'd never think they were related.

He wasn't even alive six years earlier.

Between their lack of physical resemblance and the age gap, she's never really interacted with her youngest cousin meaningfully. She's certainly not as close with him as she is with his sister. Now that she thinks about it, she doesn't think she's ever talked to him outside of a group setting.

"Hey, Jem," she says, going back to her nails. "Do you need something?"

"Is my sister coming back soon?" Jem asks shyly. Joya never realized how quiet he actually was. Guess that's her fault for never talking to him. Feeling a little guilty, she puts her nail polish down and faces him fully.

"She just left a few minutes ago, and the 7-Eleven is nearly two miles away, so she won't be back for a while," she tells him.

Jem nods slowly, and Joya expects him to go back inside, but instead, he sits next to her on the steps. He looks over at her feet curiously. "What are you *doing*?" he asks, slightly bewildered.

"I'm painting my nails. Your sister and I do it together all the time," she informs him.

She expects him to drop it and go back inside to wait for his Slurpee, but he doesn't. Instead, he keeps asking questions. "Why?"

She thinks for a moment. "Because I'm bored," she admits. There isn't much to do at Tahoe without company. "And it's a pretty color, isn't it? It looks like the trees." She lifts her foot to compare her nails to a nearby tree.

"Why didn't you go to 7-Eleven?" Jem asks, persistent despite his shy tone. Joya puts her foot back down and sighs.

"Do you want to hear a secret, Jem?" she asks him.

Like any little kid, he nods enthusiastically.

"I'm not good at riding a bike. I mean, I know *how*. I'm just not very good at it. I don't ride it very much in the city, since I take the train everywhere. I knew that I'd just slow everybody down if I went."

She expects him to ask her another *why* question. Why she isn't good at riding a bike. Why she rides the train. But instead, Jem extends his foot. "Can you paint *my* nails?" he asks. Joya is a bit surprised, but she agrees all the same. They don't talk, but it's a comfortable silence—the sort she's only accustomed to having with Ruth and Libby.

"Boys don't wear nail polish in Utah," Jem says. "But I'm glad they do in DC." Remembering how the boys in her middle school used to tease each other for doing anything feminine, Joya thinks that it's not exactly true that boys can wear nail polish there. But she doesn't want to tell the five-year-old that, so she doesn't say anything. Regardless, she bites back a smile. She would have expected to be uncomfortable by Jem's observation that she's not like the rest of the cousins. But now, it just makes her happy. She's glad that she can do something good for him by being different, even if it's something as small as painting his nails. Sure, she's not religious or white, and she's not from Utah. But she feels like she belongs because of that, not in spite of it.

From Joya's perspective, it's a very, *very* long way down. And the rocks over the side look extremely sharp.

Something pierces through her stomach, but she resists the urge to tell Ruth and Libby "No." Since they drove to Sand Harbor—without their parents for the first time, since Ruth now has her license—she's known what she wants to do.

Six years ago, she wanted more than anything to fit in, but she was too scared to force herself to jump. Now, she thinks she would be fine watching on the sidelines. It wouldn't hurt her as deeply to sit on the beach and drink a Coke as it once might have.

Now, she's not *not* scared. Doubts still persist in her head. *What if my swimsuit gets caught on the cliff? What if there's rocks below and I hit my head?* But among those doubts is no longer a keen awareness of how different she would be for not jumping. It's no longer a choice between doing what she wants and being who she wants.

With the freedom to say no without bitterness, to not participate without feeling like an outsider, she realizes that maybe she wants to jump. Maybe she wants the memory for when she goes back to DC. Maybe she wants to share this experience with her cousins. Or most likely, maybe it would just be *fun.*

She's never felt more imperfect, more alive, more like herself than as she jumps into the cold, clear water below, laughing in delight and holding Ruth and Libby's hands.

ALLIUM

Dylan Furbay

I planted rows of garlic between the divots in your corduroys

but just as the sprouts professed their green,

they died in the darkness of drawers,

bygone and buried beneath

the jeans that I've never seen you wear.

Now,

the threadbare hem drapes over your pale ankles

and the muscle has deflated from your calves.

Your face isn't full like I remember.

Those strong swells you once were

have sharpened into lean suggestions of life,

veiled by slender weeds of hair.

I miss your alien bones

distorting canvas shoes,

the meager laces tense

and smothering your feet,

but now they seem to fit you.

I thought that looking at you now

would be like cutting onions,

which I never do without my contacts

or a candle lit,

but if I cut into you,

I wouldn't need Bergamot Mist,

because your insides don't have

the enzymes to make me cry.

I planted rows of garlic between the divots in your corduroys

but I think I'll just buy some at the store.

LIKE FATHER

Libby L. Kowitz

THE MAIL TRUCK CRAWLS DOWN the street like a dog dragging its broken leg behind it, one speck of battered white against dark and gnarled trees.

I pause beside the curtains. The window is up, screen down, and the August heat burns my lungs. Dusk turns the edges of the sky black. My house is the final stop on the mail route, and I have had all day for a tight ball to form in my chest and compress my lungs as I wait for the urn to arrive.

The truck sputters to a stop in front of my lawn, beside the crooked mailbox stuck up on a rugged stake driven deep into the flesh of the ground. It's surrounded by a sea of newspapers in plastic bags that remind me of the gloves doctors wear to keep their hands clean from blood. Mom and I have not collected them in a few weeks. Dad always insisted that it was his job; he never had a reason for it, though he never had reasons for much of anything he did that I knew. It does not feel right for Mom or me to take his chore over yet.

The mailman sorts our mail, slow as a dying worm on the pavement after a storm. His skin is a pale hue, weathered with deep lines like a knobby tree. His eyes are shadows beneath protruding, bare brows. He stabs several envelopes into the mailbox and drags himself up our steep drive to the front door with a brown package in hand.

By the time he knocks, I am already at the door, opening it wide like a mouth, jutting out from the entryway like a tooth to greet him. He passes the package, jerks his thumb to the newspapers. "You should do somethin' about those," he says.

I thank him for the unsolicited advice and slam the door in his face.

I can hear his footsteps punch down the driveway, the thump of the truck's door, the yowl of the engine as he hightails it down our quickly dimming street to a less rural part of town. Where Mom and I live, it is only trees and us. I like it that way. As Dad always said, people have a habit of filling the world with hollow words instead of insight. It is only the curious who like the quiet because it is in the silence that we find answers, find what we are made of.

I find Mom curled on the couch amidst a sea of blankets and tissues. Her grief is the gaping throat of a shark, ready to devour her whole. She no longer paints her smile on each morning. She and Dad grew up together, spent so much of their lives together, that she never learned who to be without him.

At the sight of the package, she beckons me close. I sink into the couch beside her. She slices through the brown tape on the box like she is a butcher and the tape, fresh meat. The flaps of the box peel open.

Dad's urn is tucked between the shadows. It is so dark a crimson that it resembles a bullet wound. I am the one who picked it from a selection on the funeral home's website. I chose it, not because Dad would like it, but because it could hide in the shadows, concealing what it contained from prying eyes.

I suppose the urn is fitting for Dad, in that respect.

"We should put his ashes in this," Mom says. "I think I set them in the garage at his workbench." The workbench where Dad spent most of his time when he was alive felt like the only place where we would not have to reckon with the pile of dust that was left in his absence.

I stare down at my feet and toe across floorboards that groan, past the kitchen, into the garage. I remember when I was little, Dad used to grab me by the arms and drop me on his shoelaces, so I had one foot on each of his. We would walk around the house like this, feet stacked and holding hands. He would groan louder than the floorboards each time he stepped to make me feel big and old and strong. I spent so much time wishing the smallness of my childhood away. Now, the rapidly fading memories from when I was little are all I have left of him. He's gone, and it's like I don't know how to walk anymore without his socks beneath mine.

The lights in the garage come alive a few seconds later with a faint buzz that jars me from my thoughts. It reminds me of a hospital waiting room, the smell of chemicals and the haunt of all who never made it out alive hanging in the stale air.

Two of the bulbs are out, leaving only the one light above Dad's workbench on. It casts his area in a yellow glow, like the final scream of the sun before it is shoved from the sky at dusk. Dad's Mustang is parked in the center of the garage, collecting dust beside his bags of quicklime—from when he repaved the driveway himself last summer.

I squeeze past it to his workspace. He was always here, though I never knew what he was tinkering with, only that he liked the work, only that it felt like some secret all fathers must have. His workbench is an altar, the nails and wrenches and hammers, his idols. Bleeding and bruised fingertips and aching muscles were his sacrifices.

He once told me he loved nothing more than his work in this garage. I would often stow myself away inside. As if I could become the wood he carved, the tools he held, the nails he hammered away at. He took such care of the things he made, and I drank him like poison.

My most vivid memory of Dad is here. His hands stained with a grease so brown it looked like dried blood, his eyes with that wild light they caught whenever he was hard at work. At eight years old, I had crawled beneath his Mustang and watched with trepid fascination while he toiled over his space, occasionally bending to strike a mallet as if nailing the lids to coffins—though my gaze was never privy to his worship.

My dust allergies gave me away with a sneeze. Dad yanked me out by my arm, and his eyes took a red tint, like he was a memory trapped in an old photograph. His hammer slipped from his hand and hit my toe, and I howled. "Eden?" He blinked away the red. My name was all he said before he dragged me by the scruff of my neck like a feral cat inside. Neither of us spoke of it again, but I understood. There were things Dad did that were for him alone.

Even now, ten years after that happened, I still shake as I swipe through low-hanging cobwebs that catch across my mouth like stitches, dig through the bins and trays where his tools have been laid to rest. Screws. Allen wrenches. Tape measures.

There are no ashes that I can see. I remember Mom put them in one of those blue Ziploc gallon bags. Against the gray of the workbench, the taupe wood handles of the hammers, the red matchbox, and the silver nails, the blue bag should be as easy to spot as a lump protruding from smooth skin stretched over bone.

I sift through another few bins, stopping only when I stumble upon newspaper clippings beneath an assortment of hammers. The front pages feature the faces of pretty girls and headlines: *Missing* or *Found Dead*. The oldest clippings are dated before I was born, and the newest is from seven months ago, about a girl named Sally Webb.

Sally Webb was a senior at my high school last year. I only passed her in the halls a few times. She had a devoted boyfriend and friends who missed her, and a family who went on the local news channel to beg for anyone to share information. That was before they found Sally's body at the bottom of a river. It made sense to me that Dad followed that news story. Sally was a few years older than me, and I know he always worried about something happening to me.

But the rest of the clippings, with the faces of the dead or missing girls from years ago that stare up at me with smiles on their lips and eyes bright with a future they would not see, seem to have no relevancy to our lives. They are only girls who are dead or missing.

The ball in my chest tightens again. I stuff the hammers inside the plastic bins like I am stuffing intestines inside the cavity of an abdomen.

Dad's ashes are missing.

There is a part of me that wants to believe they were never here. He was never ashes. He is still sagging skin and calloused fingers, curses and spit, blood and bone. Mom is not waiting with his urn in the house for me to return with what's left of him. He got up and wandered out. All on his own. Because that is something he can still do. Maybe he went to the hardware store. Or to pick up dinner. Although his Mustang is still here. But it almost never left the garage, even when he was—

It was too precious to take outside. The Mustang. Like he was afraid he would dent it or scratch it or lose it. Maybe if I had locked him up inside this garage like he did his car, he would still be here.

But I didn't. And he isn't.

I am ready to conclude that they are forever lost somewhere I won't have to come to terms with his death when I notice the corner of a blue gallon bag in the driver's seat of his Mustang.

I tiptoe to the car. I pluck his ashes from the leather seats, slam the door shut, listen to the echo, watch the dust unsettle from the disturbance I caused until my eyes lose their focus and stare and stare and stare.

I notice the heavy shadows behind Dad's workbench.

I shake the blur out of my eyes. From this angle, I see what I had not seen before. It is not heavy shadows at all, but a hole in the wall that is mostly hidden behind his workbench. The little I can see is pitch black nothingness, a gaping chip in the wall that beckons like sleep. I imagine it as a black hole in space, ripping apart the wall, growing larger and larger to swallow everything it touches.

I blink, and my feet have pulled me steps closer to the workbench. I blink again and I am there, stuffing the ashes into my back pocket. My hands do not feel like my own, reaching around it, feeling the wall for cracks, for the hole that gapes like a gash.

In my mind, I picture all that could come from it. A bony hand reaching out to haul me inside. A portal to another world that will suck me in and drain me of life. Spiders that pool out the edges and shadow the wall with countless bodies, coat my skin and bite deep into my flesh, climb into my mouth and nose until I am choking, vision fading, lungs deflating.

Heart stopping.

Instead, my hands snag on a notebook which had been stuffed into a pocket of the wall, between insulation and wood, like the house was built around it, a ribcage curled around blackened lungs. I tug it free and wipe the dust from the leather cover. An emblem of an apple tree is carved on the front of it.

I make quick work of undoing the straps that bind it. On the first page, there is only one word: *Confessions.*

I flip through the pages. There are bends in some of the corners, little marks that remind me he was alive once. On each line there are two names and one date. A woman's name, a man's name. All in my father's messy but legible handwriting. I never thought I'd see that again. Dates ranging from before I was born to less than a year ago, in chronological order, no names that I recognize, no dates that stick out to me, until at last, I find one I know.

Sally Webb.

Beside her name, a man's name that I do not know. *Evan Morris.*

It is dated five weeks ago.

I close the book. Cradle it in my hands. Slip my fingers into the indents on the cover he left from holding it so many times. His hands were so much larger than mine. It's almost like holding him again. Almost.

I check the wall for anything else. Less than a foot from the floor, my fingers brush the tops of jars. Dozens of them, coated in layers of dust and broken wall and bits of insulation, and I remember stories of people hoarding moonshine in their houses during abolition, ready to drown in liquor to spite their government.

Somehow, I know that is not what these jars are for.

I yank one free from the stash and wiggle my arm back through the hole.

A still, bloodied heart encased in clear jelly is stuck inside it.

I drop the jar. It cracks on the floor, sending glass and jelly chunks scuttling across the concrete, beneath the workbench, into the tires of Dad's Mustang, and the heart gives a bounce, arteries and dried bits of blood smothering my socks.

I gag.

What have I done to my father's temple? That is my first thought. Not the jars. Not the journal. Not the heart. The workbench. I have made a mess of it. Something hits me right in the chest. Knowing Dad will not be there to scold me when he sees it. I wish he were here. He would never have let me see this.

Grief moves me. I collect the glass chunks until my skin is kissed with hundreds of cuts. I discard the glass in the hole in the wall, where it clangs against the remaining jars that could be full of other organs, kick the heart beneath the workbench—*anything* to scrape what I have seen from my brain, shove it back where it belongs, where I cannot see it.

If I cannot see it, I do not know about it.

I rub my hands raw on my pants, first to get the blood and jelly off, then to feel the sharp sting of the cuts against rough fabric again and again, to know that I am alive, to feel like I am still inside my body, not observing this from the outside.

The door to the garage slots open.

I jerk around. My shoulders are tight. I grip the journal as if it is a weapon, as if it could protect me, as if whatever opened the garage door is worse than the secret I have uncovered in the hole behind my father's workbench.

But the garage is empty.

And the journal is hot in my hands, and the garage is spilling light into the house, and eventually Mom will get worried enough to look for me, and my feet are already pedaling forward, stealing me away inside the house where I do not feel like I am rifling through the pieces of Dad he never wanted me to see.

I slam the garage door shut and lock it. As if that could keep the demons outside this house. I toss the ashes to Mom and beeline to the bathroom, where I scrub my hands until I am certain the smell of decay is gone, and only then do I place the journal in the dark beneath my bed. There it will stay until I decide what to do with it.

At first, it's easy to ignore it. I do not forget about it, but I can pretend it's not there. I spend my days with Mom, and neither of us has a reason to visit the garage, since it has become a graveyard for the things Dad once loved.

But in the night, I am always thinking of it. I am thinking of the father who sat on that bench, and how he was not the Dad who walked me around the house on his shoelaces. I am thinking of his wild red eyes, the downward slope of his lips. His shoulders hunched and broad, catching light and casting shadows.

The weight of my blankets crushes me into my mattress. I stare at the ceiling, wriggling my fingers and toes and forehead and lips to draw the tension out of my muscles and fall into a deep and relaxing sleep. There is only blank space above me, the ceiling like an unmarked headstone to carve my thoughts upon.

My thoughts, which are stuck on the hole and the journal and the hearts in their jars.

Dad was always drawn to his secrets. I never minded. Not until there were dozens of people in line at my father's funeral, clasping my hands, telling me their favorite stories of him, sharing the pieces of him that he shared with them, and I realized I had no stories—nothing that mattered anyway. I think it is in everyone's nature to want to know the people they came from. But I also think ugliness is the nature of truth.

I push myself onto my side and stick an arm beneath my bed, fingers fumbling for the journal. I curse under my breath for leaving it so far from my reach. But eventually, I get a firm enough grip to haul it into bed with me. It dents my cover like a hammer to the head.

I start by researching Evan Morris. It sounds like a normal, inconspicuous name, so I include *Lexington, Kentucky* in my Google search, hoping that will give me the most accurate results. I click the news tab, scroll through the headlines.

There is one that catches my eye from five months ago.

EVAN MORRIS ACQUITTED ON ALL CHARGES; FOUND NOT GUILTY.

Beside it, there is a picture of a man in a crisp funeral suit. His hair is greasy, his eyes blue and beady. His lips curl in a smirk, and he is looking at his hands, folded together on the table. There is a courtroom blurred behind him, faces I cannot see. I wonder if they are smiling like him or if his verdict builds tears in their eyes.

I click the link, skim the article, and the sight of one name stops me cold.

"Morris, who is on trial for the murder of Sarah Webb, a young senior in high school who was found dead two months ago, has been acquitted on all charges, after the jury ruled that there was insufficient evidence to convict him."

I compare the date of the article to the date in Dad's journal, but Evan Morris was acquitted months before Dad wrote his name. My attention turns to the other names in the journal. I type them in. The internet is quick to point me to murder trials for the corresponding girls and women found dead, the accused walking free each time.

But the dates they walk free and the dates in Dad's journal never match. It is like Dad logs them later, as though he hears months after the trials what the outcomes were. If all these men were acquitted, why is he keeping their names?

Why does he have jars—possibly filled with hearts—behind his workbench?

I flip through the journal. Hoping for answers. Hoping for something that tells me I knew my dad all along, that he is all the things he told me he was instead of the culmination of secrets he kept from me.

But after Sarah Webb, there are only empty pages.

I nudge the journal beneath my pillow, check the clock. It reads three in the morning, which gives me little time to sleep. I hope I wake up and realize this was all a dream, find that there is no journal beneath my pillow, and there is no hole in the garage.

Before I close my eyes, I think, briefly, that I see Evan Morris standing in my doorway.

I BEGIN TO SEE HIM everywhere.

At first, I think it's a trick of my mind. That theory is quickly buried when Dad's urn moves from the mantel to the bookshelf to the kitchen table and back, and Mom asks if I moved it, and I tell her no, and she mumbles to herself that she thought she put it on the mantel this morning. "I must have forgotten," she says. "Urns don't walk."

She means it as a joke. But the moment it is on top of the mantel, it inches across as if to spite her. Mom does not see it, and it topples off the edge, crashing to the floor, sending what is left of Dad spilling like guts, and Evan Morris is visible, an outline or silhouette more than a person, but I can see enough to catch his smirk. It is the same smirk from the photo at his trial.

Mom chalks this up to her own mistake, but I know better.

I find my hairbrush in the hallway instead of the bathroom later. My shoes are mismatched in my closet. Dresser drawers opened; clothes picked through. I see whisps of grey at the edges of my vision, notice doors swinging open. And the few times I venture out of the house, I see his face on strangers.

I always glimpse him from afar. The distance between us, the short span of which I see him is enough to make me second guess myself. The few instances where he is close enough that I could glimpse him, he is more shadow than man. I can make out a smirk, or a glint in the eyes, but he is a shadow puppet made of claws and teeth more than flesh and blood.

I hear him howling in the night. Shouts of pain and muffled cries, fists banging on my bedroom door, pleas for help that go unanswered as I burrow into my blankets, tuck my head beneath my pillow.

I have always been pale. But lately, all the color has drained from my cheeks, my eyes have sunken in and darkened. I am falling asleep during the day, only to wake to his ghost watching me from a corner of my room in the night.

Even Mom comments on my sleeping habits and restlessness. Though she is bouncing between her grief on the couch and her nursing interviews too much to do much about it. She offers to set up an appointment for me with a doctor—or a therapist. But I wave her off. I do not think either could do much about the ghost.

It is so early in the morning that the sun has not torn its way through the blackened sky yet when I return to the garage. It has a rotten smell to it now, so I dig into one of the quicklime bags and shovel the alkaline material over the heart. I remember reading that quicklime is used in burials to cover the smells of corpses, and I wonder, briefly, if my father knew that, if we had extra because these hearts came from bodies he needed to hide.

I shove that thought from my mind. This time, I am prepared. I yank on gardening gloves, reach inside the hole, and I do not drop the jars when I see the hearts—no matter how much I might want to, staring at the flaky, blood red organs forever preserved in that last beat of life. I turn off the part of my brain that wants to run, that wonders why there are so many hearts in my father's garage. I treat this like biology class. I am not in my garage; I am in a lab. These hearts are not my dad's. They belonged to cadavers, pigs, or cows. If I think for even one second about him, about the hearts and the secrets—I won't ever find out why. This is a part of him that I don't know. But it's a part no one else knew, either. It's like one last secret between us. So, I swallow my bile and pile the jars onto the workbench.

There are thirty-nine in total.

There are forty names in Dad's journal. Each jar is marked with a confession:

I, Alex Kaur, confess to killing Nicole Perry.

I, Tristan Roger, confess to killing Abby Parker.

I, Samuel George, confess to killing Amber Dean.

And a death date:

Alex Kaur, March 7, 2001.

Tristan Roger, October 30, 2007.

Samuel George, June 12, 2015.

Though the death dates are written in my father's handwriting, the confessions are not.

Each one is scrawled in its own handwriting. Alex Kaur writes in cursive. Tristan Roger skips the dot over his *i*. Samuel George's *e*'s are missing the tail at the bottom. I have no doubt in my mind; these men wrote these confessions themselves.

My stomach twists into knots. *Confessions.* That is what my father meant—he did what the courts could not do. He found these men who were released, and drew confessions from their lips, and hearts from their chests. Thirty-nine hearts, all the names in his journal accounted for, except for Evan Morris, whose heart is beneath the workbench, covered in quicklime.

I do not know whether to call Dad a hero or a monster. These men were found innocent, and yet he proved them guilty. These girls were murdered, and he brought them justice. Justice they were never getting—no one can be tried twice for the same crime. But.

But he went after these men.

But he killed them.

But he kept their hearts.

The Mustang's lights kick on. I hear the engine rev. I have seconds to plaster myself against the wall before it barrels from a standstill into my father's workbench, and I see him, Evan Morris, leering at me from the driver's seat. Jars topple and smack into the concrete, hearts ricochet across the hood of the car, and bits of jelly slick the floor.

For the first time, I can see Evan Morris. He is not an outline or a silhouette, but an echo of a person. His shirt is torn to show wide, bloodied gashes along his torso. His alabaster skin is shredded in places—and I wonder if it is rot from the decay of his body that came after death, or if my father flayed his skin from bone to draw a confession from him.

Evan Morris puts the car into gear.

My mother, who had not heard his cries or howls, or the banging on my door late in the nights, shouts, "Is everything okay?" and Evan Morris is momentarily still.

She can hear him, I realize. This time, she can hear him. I see it dawn on his face too. The wide eyes, the blink, the lips that stretch into that god-awful smirk of his. He is paying me no mind, giving me the chance to inch along the wall, closer to the door, when I hear her footsteps. My eyes cut to the hearts.

Mom can't find out. She has always been fragile. Consumed now with grief over the man she spent her whole life loving. But the man she loved was a figment. She is not strong enough to love the person he was behind his mask. She is not me.

I shout, "Fine. I just dropped something."

Mom yells again, telling me that she is leaving for an interview, and that she will be gone most of today. I hear her footsteps tread to the front door; I hear it slam shut and lock behind her. I listen for her car as it backs from the driveway and leaves me stranded with this ghost.

This ghost who is staring at me.

Not me.

Past me.

His eyes are on the jars of hearts, the few still intact on Dad's workbench, and I wonder, if I was a ghost who had been murdered, if I was haunting the place I was killed, what is it I would want? Revenge? I couldn't get it. Not on a dead man. Maybe on his family. But more than that, I would want people to know how I suffered.

I would want them to see the hearts my killer collected.

I would want justice.

And he'll kill me to get it.

My father isn't here to protect his secrets anymore. But I am.

The car is rolling back, denting the garage, shifting gears, speeding toward me, and I lunge. My fingers fumble for the matchbox on Dad's workbench. I strike one, two, three matches in the span of seconds, tossing one into the car, one onto the slick floor, one onto the workbench.

The car slams into me.

The floor erupts in flames.

My vision goes dark around the edges, and I crumble. There are sharp splinters of pain in my hips and ribs, but I do not feel them, not really. I am both aware and slipping out of my body. My hands are pressed into the lit, jellied floor, fingertips singed with the fire I started. I watch it engulf the walls, spread to the door.

The house is burning.

I push myself to my knees. My vision swims. I shove myself across the hood and cross the stretch between me and the garage door opener. I slam my fist against the button and hear the chains above me groan. The car engine revs again. The garage crawls, giving me an inch, four, seven— and Evan Morris switches gears.

He is putting the car in reverse. My thoughts are scattered; it takes me precious seconds to realize that if he backs the car into the garage door, it will break, and I will be stuck here with him, inhaling the smoke, burning in the flames.

He presses his foot to the gas.

I roll under the door. It shudders and drops and hits my shoulder. I yelp. Bloodied, burned hands press into the metal end as it cuts into me like the scythe of a reaper, until I have hauled it up enough to roll completely out of harm's way, and into my driveway.

It slams shut behind me.

A moment later, Evan Morris walks through. The echo of flesh on his face sags and melts, his skin peels, and his clothes fall into a puddle at his feet. I watch him reach for me. I watch the bones disintegrate one by one into dust before getting whipped away by wind.

I watch his ghost vanish.

Somewhere in the back corners of my mind, I realize I am hot. I look to the house. The open windows vomit smoke, flames climb like orange and red snakes.

I crawl the little distance down my driveway into the street, pulling my knees to my chest, I watch my house burn like a body.

Some secrets are best left undiscovered.

A CALENDAR OF SOLAR & LUNAR ECLIPSES

Emily Sun Li

October / it's 中秋节 and the moon is full / my father buys

mooncakes from the Asian grocery supermarket (along with

napa cabbage and fish tofu, my mother's request) / my sisters

and I eat three / though our tongues prefer candy corn to

salted egg yolk / we return to our homework and costumes

late November / the day after Thanksgiving / the women

of the household make steamed 包子 stuffed with leftover

turkey, which we freeze in gallon Ziploc bags and fry for

breakfast until Christmas day / the flour on the counter

is covered with our fingerprints and they all look the same

New Year's Eve / my parents entertain guests downstairs /

their names mispronounced / a pile of shoes by the door /

distracted, they pretend not to notice my grandparents take

my sister and I to their room for a game of 麻将 / we are

mid-round when the ball drops in Times Square and I

don't hear the champagne pop over the clinking of tiles

late February / if the Lunar New Year falls on a weekend,

the family gathers at my grandparents' home in Queens /

everyone is in Valentine red and the kids sneak away from

the gelatinous delicacies we can only name in Mandarin

and the 白酒 toasts of the adult table to play Monopoly

in the attic / our pockets stuffed full with red envelopes

late February / if it's a weekday, I'm at school / my Asian

friends and I order Chinese takeout and tip the driver 30% /

we FaceTime our families in broken Chinglish and

raise our pearl milk teas to the new year and to us—

      to decades spent celebrating only day or night /

      to yellow and bronze and honey and freckled gold,

our skin shining every shade of reflected light /

to the way we constantly, casually

rearrange the cosmos to make sun & moon

    & Earth & us

   align

JUST ANOTHER HEARTBREAK PLOT

Ashley Diers

WHEN ONE IS SUFFERING FROM being spurned by the object of their affection, it is customary, I suppose, to bury lingering feelings of rejection in ice cream or hobbies. I prefer to bury mine in the ground.

Unless that counts as a hobby. And after the third burial (James Winters, cause of death: failure to exchange numbers or any other identifying information once camp ended), maybe it does.

I wedge the shovel into the dirt one final time. "Here lies my feelings for Trevor Hindley. You know what they say, the best friend of my best friend's boyfriend is destined to be my boyfriend."

Or so I desperately *wanted* him to be. If, after Frida successfully asked us to prom, we hadn't shared merely one dance and even fewer words.

So here I am, in the middle of Tower Park, burying yet another would-be love interest, with the old "Witch's Hat" water tower as my only witness. The perfect picture of a mourning widow in my fascinator hat with the delicate netting and black, gauzy babydoll dress. Though, perhaps, my heeled boots in a soft lavender, and pastel bracelets lining my arms are a bit more whimsical than traditional funeral attire. Not that this is traditional to anyone but me and Frida.

"The thing about Trevor I will always remember is tagging along to Frida and Brody's date, then baking cookies together instead of watching the Super Bowl." I light the (cocoa and cinnamon scented) candle, any chances of a relationship going up in flames with the paper bearing Trevor's name. Hopefully, I've also managed to extinguish the last of my shame at all the topics I rambled about between then and prom, which I fear may have contributed to disintegrating my dating dreams.

Nevertheless, I mourn our definitely-not-love affair.

"And though I maintain we would've worked out perfectly, our time together was tragically cut short—" I pause, mound of dirt in hand, noticing a boy casting a shadow over me. An unwittingly *cute* boy… who's just caught me in the act of burying a freaking piece of paper. Neat. Love that for me.

"Sorry. I came to read by my favorite—usually lonely—tree." He gestures toward the scraggly, crooked branches overhead with the tattered paperback in his hand. "Don't mind me." The boy walks backwards with a crescent-moon grin, golden curls glowing like a halo in the sun.

But instead of, I don't know, picking a different place to read and leaving me to complete my ritual in peace, he just…sits. Opening the pages of a mystery book, the cover half-missing and the spine so creased the title is hardly visible.

The dirt slips between my fingers, cascading to the ground. I can't possibly resume my whole unusual ceremonial thing *now*. With this boy so close. Even if he is ostensibly reading. I *knew* I shouldn't have attempted this alone. Why, oh why, couldn't I have just sat with my feelings for one more week until Frida came back from vacation?

This is so much worse than the time my crush on Zack Deighton (born of physics lab partner stars aligning), was pronounced dead on the scene after Frida saw him at the mall and told him (against my implicit wishes and her better judgment) that I thought he was hot and his response was, "Oh. Thanks." Not: "She's pretty cute, too." Not: "Tell her hi and hey, I was wondering, would she want to hang out some time?" Just, "Thanks." RIP me, actually.

The boy looks up like he can feel the weight of my burning stare as strongly as I can feel his presence, sending me to an early grave. "Really, no need to stop on my account." His gaze flickers between me and the candle barely visible around the scattered dirt pile. "But I am dying to know what exactly you're doing."

I *should* just pack up and leave. The important part—destroy all evidence of who I dared to like—has already been completed. I'm in no way obligated to confess my truth to this literal stranger. I could tell him to move along. Nothing to see here. Just another heartbreak plot.

But maybe it's morbid curiosity of my own that roots me in place, attempting an emotionless air to explain. "I liked someone. He didn't like me. I don't want to think about him anymore. So I'm burying my feelings." I nod toward the anthill of paper ashes. "Literally. Why?" I find myself sardonically asking, as he observes me smoothing the ground with my shovel. "Did you want to say some words?"

"I'd love to." He tucks the book into his pocket, now fully invested as he kneels next to me, adopting a solemn look and demeanor. "Here lies a dearly departed soul. Beloved by this girl. Their love affair, as I understand it, was tragically cut short. As such, his only crime was…"

He trails off, stage-whispering while trying not to break his serious façade. "What was his crime?"

I stare at my hands, brushing remnants of dirt away. "We went to prom together but never hung out or talked afterward."

He waits a few beats like I'm supposed to say more before realizing I'm not going to. "That's it? That was his only crime?"

I struggle not to laugh incredulously. "I didn't say he committed any crimes. *You* did. *I* simply wanted to get over him once and for all so I don't spend all summer pining after someone who doesn't want me. This is how I do it."

"Fascinating," he says like he earnestly means it. Which, I'm disconcerted to find, pulls at my heartstrings with the smallest inklings of a crush. An unlikely one, the others typically falling under the sullen and brooding category. "And how many, uh, funerals—"

"Heartbreak plots," I correct. That's what Frida calls them. The name seemed more unique and somehow less ridiculous than "boy burials."

"Heartbreak plots, then. How many have you…dug?"

I bite back another laugh at him tripping over the wording, confessing my body count.

"And how long have you been doing this?" he asks.

"Since this failed crush I had as a freshman? And I'll be a senior next year, so…"

"Wow. Seven people in two years—"

"Six."

He levels a glance at me as if silently challenging me to explain.

Yeahhhhh. Dylan Venturi (born of sophomore year marching band, died (the first time) the day concert band chairs were announced and he asked me out, reneging before we actually did) required multiple symbolic burials. That sucker kept coming back to life like a freaking member of the undead—only a way less hot and charming vampire, at that. Thus, even more baffling in his ability to keep popping into my feelings.

But I refuse to tell this random boy all of that. Suffice to say, I gloss over the gory details of how Dylan was eventually willing to be with me—as a friends with benefits situation—no thanks—by implying it was an on-again-off-again sort of thing.

"Still. You're practically a serial killer of heartbreaking, huh?" He flashes a disarmingly dimpled half grin.

"Not really." More like serially heartbroken.

He nods at my non-elaboration. "So, how did this whole thing start? You just woke up one day and decided, 'I'm done with him, time to hit up the park and turn it into a personal cemetery?'"

"You know, I don't have to give you information if you're going to judge."

That's what Bradley Bennett did when I made the mistake of only half-jokingly mentioning what my weekend plans entailed. Of course, maybe it's for the best he never became a true crush if at fifteen years of age he *actually* thought I was capable of cursing him. Please. He wasn't even monumental enough to be worth a heartbreak plot, let alone wasting a curse on him if I did possess magical powers.

"No judgment here." He holds his hands up in surrender. "Just a healthy sense of curiosity."

"Some could call it unhealthy," I say dryly.

"Because it's definitely healthy to bury every crush you've ever had?" A full display of dimples and a teasing tone make an appearance.

"Do you ask this many questions to every stranger you meet?" I deflect to cover the feelings building in my chest, unfortunately intrigued.

"Only the cute, interesting ones grieving their exes. I crash those funerals with my inquisitiveness all the time."

Oh, no. There it is. I'm a goner. Fastest crush to form, fastest to die.

And if this glimmer of affection is all it takes to make me confess the whole (mostly) unabridged history of my heartbreak plots, so what? What's he going to do if he's weirded out? Never speak to me again? I'm operating under the assumption that's already the case.

So I cave. Starting from the beginning. "Alright, it's freshman year. I'm in Drawing 101 when this guy chooses to sit next to me. Turns out he's a senior—"

"A senior?" The boy looks skeptical. Likely already putting together the reason for the crush's timely death: separation by graduation—his.

Yes, Jonas Longland was a senior. Yes, I was a freshman. Yes, I *do* see how we would've had a 0.001 percent chance of actually working out even if he did like me. *Now.* But at the time all I knew was how I felt when he studied every inch of my face for a semester. How was I not supposed to fall at least *half* in love with him? I mean, come on.

I continue to explain the circumstances of my crushes and their demises. He stops me when I reach the penultimate one before today's crashed "funeral." Heartbreak Plot Number Six: Levi Emerson.

"And what happened to him? It was over the moment you found out he hates cats?"

I shake my head with a small smile.

"Hmm. You…hated the way he always asked you to help him with his homework?"

Close. Except, embarrassingly, I *loved* that about him. I casually say, "Oh, you know. We stopped having chemistry together."

"Ah." A sage, pensive nod. "Been there."

This is where Frida's voice comes to mind, snorting and adamantly insisting I stop phrasing it like that, otherwise people will get the wrong idea. Which is…fair. So, sheepishly, I admit, "No. Literally.

We stopped having chemistry *class* together. End of close proximity, end of crush."

"And none of these crushes have ended in a relationship?"

"Sadly, no," I lament. "Apparently nobody's ever had feelings for me. Ergo, this." I gesture at the ground in front of me.

"Have you ever considered, you know, putting yourself out there? Telling any of these guys how you feel? Instead of just assuming the worst?"

"What? No. I could never."

He gives me a searching look. "Then for all you know any of them could have been harboring feelings and holding their own burials for you."

I fiddle with the beads on my bracelet, rifling through the headstones in my mental graveyard for any chance that he could be right. Zack? Obviously not. Dylan? Another hard no. James…was a maybe. Except I could never quite tell if he liked me or another girl in my cabin. Same with Levi, who flirted with me often enough to make me question the possibility of us—until he acted the same with every other girl in class. "I…that's doubtful."

"Still, in order for anything to happen, *someone* has to step up and say something for the relationship part to happen, right? Why *couldn't* it be you?"

"Because…" I stare at the candle's flame dancing in the wind. "What if I was rejected on the spot? I'd have to dig my own grave then."

He doesn't laugh. Instead, he prods further. "You're telling me you never gave anyone a chance out of fear?"

"So? Again, nobody has confessed to liking me, either. Some of them actually made their lack of feelings quite clear in their actions." Dylan certainly did when the late-night texts—along with our entire friendship—ceased. Hammering the final nail into that particular coffin.

But instead of admitting that, I go on the offense.

"And what about you? If it's really so easy, enlighten me how you've asked out every single person *you've* ever liked." He winces but doesn't protest. "Yeah. I thought not. Then can you honestly tell me you've *never* had someone you'd love to cast aside? Someone you wanted to kill your feelings for by any means possible? Even if, yeah, that means pretending they're dead to you?"

We're both silent after my accidental outburst of passion. I half expect him to leave. I mean, I did just launch a (largely unprompted) barrage of attacks with no chance to defend himself. He has no reason not to turn away and never look back. His quiet inspection is worse than if he had.

Well, that's it, I suppose. I glance at my watch to officially call it. Time of death: 1:15 p.m. Good thing I didn't develop *actual* feelings for him, so the mourning process should be quick and painless.

Finally, (at 1:18 p.m.), he says, "You're right. I do have someone like that."

"Let me guess..." I pause to brainstorm fake details of his own backstory in efforts to lighten the moment and pull a laugh from him. "She was the literal girl next door until you kissed in your car one night. You dated a blissful year before deciding to go back to being friends and you became the one that got away."

He half smiles—no dimples to be seen. "You forgot the part where she woke up one day and fell out of love with me."

Oh. It's like his words have wounded me. My vulnerabilities are incredibly minuscule in comparison. Like, here I am playing pretend widow mourning silly little crushes when he's been in actual love. Frida often calls me The Girl Who Cried Unrequited Love. A nickname that doesn't usually sting. Until now.

Sorry doesn't even begin to cover it, but I say it anyway.

"It's whatever." A shrug. "Life moves on."

"And have you?" I ask tentatively, recognizing the attempted-but-not-actually-pulling-it-off casual tone. "Moved on?"

Another moment's silence follows, but it's less awkward, more that he's choosing his next words carefully. "Not yet. But I'm trying to." A smirk slides across his face. He really does have a beautiful smile. "Maybe I could try your method."

He's kidding. Surely. Jokingly indulging me as a peace offering to validate my never-ending unrequited feelings.

Except he nods toward the supplies spilling out of my cat-shaped bag. "Well?"

This is a first.

"You have to take it seriously," I say slowly, coming out of my surprise. I'm so far out of my usual realm here. I glance at him, gauging his sincerity, waiting for him to object. "It's supposed to be cathartic."

"I will." He holds up a hand, smile falling in place to say, "Let's hex her!"

"It's not a hex thing." I shake my head, reluctantly amused. "For me it's more like…banishing someone from my thoughts. An exorcism, if anything."

Another smirk. "*Hex*orcism."

"Taking it seriously?" I remind him with a smile.

"Right." He resumes his solemn look. "So, what first?"

Feeling extremely self-conscious, I take out a stack of tea-stained papers I dyed to mimic parchment.

"No judgments," I say at his look of glee as he plays with the feathery ink pen I hand over.

"No judgments," he repeats. And admittedly, he does sound reverent as he says, "Just honest fascination. I mean, who even *owns* a full-on quill, let alone carries it with them? Unless…" He side-eyes me. "You sure you aren't an actual witch?"

"Let me work my magic and find out." I flush as I realize that sounded flirtier than intended, so I overcompensate by too-quickly shoving a piece of paper at him and insisting he write down her name.

He takes his time, writing with deliberate care, not dashing off an impatient scrawl. I'm startled by my sheer curiosity as I fight the sudden, compelling need to peek, to memorize the name to stalk online later and…and what? Get more information on this soon-to-be-dead crush? Pointless.

He sets the quill down after one final flourish, bringing me back to my senses. "Now what?"

"Now, we've reached the point you so rudely interrupted earlier."

"Or was it *you* who rudely interrupted my reading?"

I fight a grin, walking him through the remaining steps.

He ticks them off on his fingers. "Light the flame, engulf the name, bury your shame. Got it." Tilting his head, he adds, "It's not the most magical of incantations, but I'll play your…game."

I pointedly ignore the butterflies flying about my stomach. "You know, I *was* going to let you give your eulogy silently, but now I've reconsidered."

He sighs in fake annoyance. "I suppose this is your area of *hex*pertise, after all. Wouldn't want to mess with the process."

"Exactly." I don't bother to correct his witchy assumptions. Or hide my smile. Though it fades as I busy myself lining up the candles while he writes a eulogy. The action gives my attention somewhere else to focus on as I brace to hear the sordid details of his relationship. Am I really capable of keeping my jealousy in check about the fact that he's loved someone before? That he's *been* loved before?

Maybe I should've been working on creating and testing love-summoning spells instead.

"This isn't reassuring me you're *not* secretly a witch." His voice cuts into my thoughts. "I'm actually confident that either your bag has a charm to make it hold more than it appears, or you can make candles appear out of thin air." He gestures at what some could consider an indie bookstore inventory's worth sitting in a row.

"What? I like to have all my options with me. Each burial requires a different scent, one specific enough to instantly transport you to special moments or places. That way when the flame is extinguished, it's like the memories and feelings symbolically evaporate too."

Dylan was autumn leaves and freshly cut grass that felt like being on the field. James was bonfire and blueberry muffins, recreating our camp breakfast staple. Jonas was ink and paper, reminiscent of the drawing pads we pored over all semester.

"That makes sense, actually. May I?" He reaches toward a lavender and rain candle, unscrewing the lid when I nod. He wrinkles his nose and repeats the process, abandoning chai latte and croissants after a few seconds of measured consideration.

I try not to glow at how seriously he's taking the whole endeavor. Even Frida hasn't put forth this much effort since Dylan's first burial. And that was five heartbreak plots ago.

I assumed it would be weird to let anyone in, but it feels inexplicably nice to be vindicated by this boy. Even if he remains a stranger, never having gotten his name. It's probably too late to ask now. I guess it'll be an unmarked grave for him when this crush inevitably dies.

The thought that he'll soon be just another heartbreak plot hurts more than it should. Because as much as I wanted to stamp out my suspiciously fast feelings developing, that's so not happening.

When he lands on a cherry blossom and sea salt candle, his eyes close, lingering on it uneasily. After a moment he shakes his head like he's clearing the fog of a memory. "This one. It's eerily similar to her favorite perfume. Uncomfortably so."

"Then it's done its job."

"See? You're obviously also a psychic and this is actually a potion you conjured up on the spot."

"You caught me."

He smiles at me in a heart stopping way before I break the moment, adapting a mysterious, low tone for ridiculous effect to ask if he's ready to complete the ritual.

I strike a match, hands shaking unnoticeably—please, please let it be unnoticeably—as he angles the wick toward me and I attempt to get the paper to catch fire without either of us getting burned.

He glances down at the words in front of him, but only once. Like that's all it takes for him to commit them to memory.

"What can I say about Lisa? She was kind. She was fun. She broke my heart. But" —his eyes flit to mine with a smile— "it'll mend."

I watch as he shovels dirt over the paper's remains, too stunned to speak.

While it's all nice and good that *his* heart's on the mend, I'm pretty sure mine just swelled and burst. I'm surprised he didn't get hit with the shrapnel.

Where do we even go from here? Seriously. What are the odds my first (potentially!) requited crush is on a stranger who I'll likely never see again. It's *definitely* too awkward to ask his name now, right?

His phone chimes, disrupting our quiet wake. He frowns, getting up to leave.

Yup. Too late now. Another missed opportunity for me.

"Well, it was nice burying my feelings with you…" A pause. "Wait, I didn't actually get your name. Please tell me it's Wednesday."

"Only if you tell me yours is something equally old-fashioned. Like Percival or Thaddeus."

He places a hand to his chest, mock offended. "Is that what you really think of me? And here I thought I was special. That you didn't bury your feelings with anyone while you were secretly hoping a Victorian ghost would come along."

"I don't think that," I say softly. "Thank you."

He nods, accepting my earnest gratitude, before continuing to joyously suggest ancient pop culture witches from Glinda to one of the Sanderson Sisters to Willow from *Buffy the Vampire Slayer*.

Once again leaving me questioning: who is this cute stranger-boy who embraces my weirdness and banters wittily like we're in a gothy rom-com?

"Sorry to disappoint with my normalcy, but it's just Madison."

"Madison." My heart tumbles as he cocks his head and gazes at me, trying several nickname variations in attempts to make it make sense. "Nope. Doesn't fit your vibe. You'll forever be known to me as Sabrina. The Teenage Witch of Heartbreak Recovery."

And with that, he flashes a final grin, wordlessly hands me a scrap of paper, and turns away. My heart tunnels six feet under the ground as I put the name—Cole—to the person retreating.

When he's out of sight, I pick up the candle I mentally selected earlier—oak leaves like the ones his favorite tree bears and old books like the worn paperback that brought him into my life—and get to work on my mourning process.

"I never thought I would meet someone who maybe, somewhat impossibly, liked me right off the bat. Someone who…understands me."

Understood me.

I'm disarmed to find myself choked up at the past tenseness of it all. Which is…odd. To say the least. For all the theatrics and spectacle of this whole ritual, that's never happened before.

I inhale shakily, starting again. "Someone who saw me. Someone who—

A gust of wind makes the paper flutter out of my hands, startling any tears away.

I narrowly avoid starting a forest fire while running past the candle in my mad dash to grab the paper, fingers closing around the torn edge. My triumphant moment is made a little less so as I'm lying flat on my back in the grass, clutching to my heart what I now realize is a page from the book he carried. I grip it like someone's about to come along and bury me with it.

I lift the paper to the sky, staring at the name again, rays of sun filtering through the trees, lighting up his handwriting—including words on the opposite side.

My breath catches as I read the previously hidden message, embers of hope glowing in my chest.

In case you'd rather not bury this one

I reread the words with the string of numbers scrawled underneath several times, as if imprinting them on my heart before they fade.

I pocket the paper, blow out the candle, and pick up my phone.

SELECTED POEMS BY AMANDA THOMAS

at the shore

my love turns & turns back to me.

a plastic bag adrift:

it reaches my feet &

lumps wet like seaweed.

not returned, but thrown.   off a cliff.

some distant coastal kid.

my agonised words are forgotten. careless hands tend

my careful love.

        used to rough work, I can't blame them.

but I won't crawl on my knees.

        sometimes it feels like I've swallowed   a clam shell,

it sits in my throat. it wants

        to yammer back out. I tell it   *hush.*

                I've had to learn to give & to take.

                not

        too much rope.

they'll choke you with it, if you let 'em.

        sailor's hands.

        will tie you up tight.

                we are stuck like maggots to our light

        sources of grief.

I fester in it. I grow.

                the slant of the moon on the sea allures.

I am jellyfish hacked   & left in blobs by the tide,

        beautiful soaking in

the precious night.

I envy the sand crabs their finger-jabbed homes.

I wonder if I wade in, will this sea carry

me away, will its salt scour me new.

In Your Hands

Love like the stun of helicopter blades.

Love like a bite—

into sweet mandarin.

Love like sonnets like Shakespeare like Austen.

Love like a Toyota Corolla.

Love like devotion & my grandmother's hands.

Love like devotion & my grandfather's hands.

Love like a gasoline leak.

Love like patriotism—

with its sinister seed.

Love like an egg—

hard to crack.

Love like the butter to my bread.

Love like one thought in two heads.

Love like crochet. Love like a chore.

Love like a slow cooker.

That makes lasagne!

Love like fear—

of my mother dying.

Love like firecracker.

Love like the epilogue to grief.

Love like a desert mirage.

Love like kept receipts.

Love at daybreak. Love at noon.

Love like a cactus—

weeping sap from its wounds.

Love like a hook—

in an '80s pop song.

Love like nerves.

Love like I never love myself.

Love—

like Jesus like sacrifice.

Love like a country twang.

Love it till it breaks—

in your hands.

My browness is a gift

In ten years, you'll beg my mother for the recipe.

You won't scrunch up your nose

at my chicken korma or dahl, question the "weird sticks"

(clove, cardamom, star anise)

in my biryani, the chapati I tear

with my bare hands.

You won't mock the smell

of turmeric & spices that cling

to my skin (a luxury I own like velvet).

You'll line up for Indian take-out.

You'll delight in the masala that burns

your Western tongue.

Soon enough, you'll choke on your words.
You won't be able to get enough

of turmeric lattes, chai, henna,

bindis & ghaghara cholis

(which you'll don, then rip off, like a costume).

You won't remember our lunch breaks at school

when you compared your tans to the other girls,

never once breathing a kind

word for dark-skinned beauty.

Now, you sigh at coconut fragrance in glossy locks.

You're oblivious to the knowledge carried

down through generations, our

braided secret

(I treasure it like I treasure my

mother's Indian gold).

Even before you were born, we

have always danced through streets, anointed

in jasmine & coconut oil, bells singing

from our ankles, brown

wrists flicked up to heaven.

RECORDS ROOM

De Elizabeth

MARGOT PERCY-QUAID CAN'T STOP THINKING about blood.

The canvas is at fault, not the flashing neurons inside her brain. It's the way the white surface turns redder and redder with each heavy stroke of her angled brush, blossoms of poppies bursting to life at the painting's edge. She sits rigid at the easel beneath the window in Room 13W, black skirt pooled around her calves, and repeatedly slashes the crimson-stained bristles against the material. Each painted petal reminds her of broken capillaries or seeping, oozing wounds. Delicate flesh, permanently stained ruby. She sweeps and stirs her brush, not thinking of art class or Headmistress Prue or this week's assignment. She doesn't think about getting an A. Doesn't think about what her classmates will say when it's time for the first roundtable critique of the semester.

Instead, Margot covers her canvas with scarlet and tastes metal and glass on her tongue.

She paints until sundown, until her pale fingers grow raw, skin peeling and swollen. Until the flowers look less like poppies and more like the whispered silhouette of a girl she once knew.

Dropping her brush to the paint-stained floor, Margot cuts a hard stare to the arched doorway. If she listens hard enough, the heavy silence almost takes the shape of a question.

Who are you drawing, Margot?

How do you know her?

Where did she go?

"THE RULES OF A TRUE art critique," Headmistress Prue clips as she paces the small studio, "is that all comments are valid. The hallowed halls of this historic building are not meant to hold filtered, sanitized thoughts." Her modest heels clack on marble, velvet black skirt trailing behind. A wisp of muted light spills overhead from the stained glass window. "No one owes you any kindness in my classroom."

Margot's mouth is dry as she stares at the row of canvases at the front of the room. A painting of a boy, holding a kite. An elderly woman with creases in her face like dough. A woman with warm brown skin and box braids.

Her stomach sours. *Portraits.* The assignment was portraits. And she painted—

Headmistress comes to a standstill in front of Margot's canvas. The pop of her heels gives way to flattened silence. The older woman's drawn-on brows dip in a practiced scowl.

Whorls of brushstrokes map the entire surface where Margot had intended to show a luminous field of poppies. Last night, she thought she painted a face. Thought she'd painted *her* again.

But all she did was make a mess of red.

"Whose assignment is this?" Headmistress Prue barks, turning slowly to the small class of Erebus University students, a mix of first-and-second-years. Margot studies her classmates, some in black blazers and scarlet bowties, others wearing white blouses and onyx pleated skirts. A dozen or so pairs of eyes stare back, nervous gazes volleying across the tightly packed studio.

"I won't ask a third time," Headmistress calls, pointing a gnarled, talon-tipped finger at the painting. "Who—"

"It's mine," Margot hears herself say.

The shift in the air is palpable. It has weight, has teeth.

"You didn't follow the guidelines," Headmistress scolds. "Have you familiarized yourself with the Erebus Student Handbook, Miss Percy-Quaid?"

Margot swallows; a blade of anxiety scrapes at the back of her throat. "Yes, Headmistress."

"Prospective art majors who don't complete their assignments are not able to participate in critique," she continues. "You may see yourself out."

Shame widens beneath Margot's ribs. The heat of her classmates' stares burns into her spine as she stands on shaking ankles, patent leather Mary Janes snapping on the marble. That dusty shard of light widens over the canvases as the sun yawns, illuminating her mistake. Embarrassment clings to her like a leech.

"You can take *that* with you," Headmistress says, gesturing. "And come back when you've painted me something new."

Margot collects the red painting, clutching it to her chest as she weaves through the row of worn desks. The other students' whispers curl around her like a cloak, crackling and sizzling. *Margot's the one I told you about,* someone hisses. *The one with the dead girlfriend.*

Margot's shoes clatter faster as she scurries toward the exit.

Margot hasn't talked to anyone since the semester started.

Heart pounding, she reaches for the door.

Margot doesn't belong here.

She flies into the hall, but not before hearing the rest of it.

Margot will never belong anywhere.

MARGOT'S PULSE IS STILL HUMMING when she reaches the phone booth outside the student center.

Folding the door shut, she presses her forehead against the glass, letting it fog beneath her stuttering breath. Still grasping the dried painting, she reaches for the black phone—the only one available for student use, located in the middle of a sprawling lawn, framed by feathery-tipped weeping willows.

Palms damp with sweat, Margot dials a number she knows by heart. As it rings, she squints at a stone building atop a squat hill in the distance, its roof swallowed by a layer of stale fog. Two large gargoyles flank either side of the entrance, mouths frozen in gaping screams to reveal sharp fangs and forked tongues. The area beneath her collar shivers with an itch as she stares. Margot fleetingly imagines the soft fibers of spiders' legs tickling her skin, and she instinctively scratches at the flesh.

The phone line clicks.

"Hello?" Margot's mother's voice is caked with static.

"Mom," her response rushes out. "Mom, I can't stay here. I know Erebus is the best art school in California, but the teachers are horrible, and—"

"Hello?"

Margot's forehead knits in a frown. "Mom, it's me. Can you hear me? Mom? *Mom—?*"

A knock on the glass sends a jolt through her bones.

A boy from Headmistress's art class stands on the other side, black blazer slung over one arm. He jabs a finger toward the phone.

"Are you almost done? Need to make a call."

Averting her gaze, Margot tries one last time. "Mom? Is this connection bad?"

The fuzzy dial tone breathes back at her.

With a sigh, Margot hangs up and tugs the door open. "Sorry. This phone doesn't work."

"Ah." The boy smirks. "You're new."

Margot narrows her eyes. "Oh? Is the telephone part of a hazing ritual?"

His smirk deepens. A dimple winks in his tan skin. "Kind of." He shifts his messenger bag to his other shoulder, holding out a hand. "Adrian Vargas. Second-year."

She hesitates for a beat. "Margot Percy-Quaid. First."

"Kicked out of Headmistress Prue's class, weren't you?" He shrugs. "A rite of passage."

"Did she do the same thing to you?"

Adrian flashes his teeth. "No, not me. *I'm* perfect."

Margot slumps against the wall of the booth, pressing the painting tighter to her blouse. Her pout only makes Adrian's Cheshire Cat grin widen.

"Cheer up, P-Q. Once you get the boot from Headmistress, things can only get better."

"P-Q?" she echoes.

"Well, Percy-Quaid is quite a mouthful."

"Oh." Her cheeks redden.

"Anyway." Adrian points to the phone again. "You mind?"

Margot relents, switching places with him, trying not to notice when her chest brushes his as they pass through the narrow opening. She untucks a lock of dark hair from behind her ear, hoping it hides the blush in her ivory skin, and darts another glance toward the gargoyles.

Her neck starts to itch again.

"Hey." Margot wedges a foot into the phone booth before Adrian can fold the door closed. "What's that building?"

His dark eyes follow hers to the stone fortress atop the hill.

"Don't go in there."

Margot swoops her stare back to his, searching for a sign that he's joking. But Adrian's smirk has vanished.

"What? Why—?"

"Just fucking with you." His mouth splits in a new smile. "But for real, you can't go in that building until you officially matriculate. It's an Erebus thing."

"What—?"

"I really gotta make this call, P-Q." Adrian flicks a glance down to her clavicle. "And *you* should go to the infirmary about…whatever you've got going on there."

Margot swings her gaze to where her black almond-shaped nails had been absentmindedly scratching at her neck this whole time.

No—not scratching.

Digging into her flesh.

She gasps through her teeth as bright blood seeps through her ruffled, snow-colored blouse.

"Oh, shit—"

Margot whirls, and breaks into a run toward her dormitory, Adrian's warning about the stone fortress forgotten.

It's only when she's standing in the dingy light of her bathroom, pressing a cold towel to her torn-up skin that she realizes:

She forgot to ask him about the trick to getting the telephone to connect.

RAIN CLAWS AT THE THICK windows later that evening as Margot sits alone in the hushed shadows of her dorm, staring at her painting of poppies.

In the darkness, it's just a smear of red. But with every knife-shard of lightning that spills into the narrow space, she sees her.

Rowena.

Each brush stroke seems to form the shape of her copper hair, the dip of her nose, the slice of her cheekbones. The shading spills together to construct her willowy limbs, the softness of her curves. Rowena fucking Gibson is everywhere in this painting, staring back at Margot with soulless eyes as if to say *I used to love you.*

Margot fingers the frayed edges of the Band-Aid on her clavicle, spine flush with cold brick. She tilts her head this way and that, studying the painting, the barest glimpses at a girl she used to know. A girl she kissed beneath an empty summer sky, a girl she whispered secrets to amid saturated twilight.

A girl who was lowered into the gaping earth while Margot watched, dressed all in black and with a gaze like stone.

Rowena, Rowena, Rowena.

She'll never forget her face. She *loved* her face. Her freckles, her perfect eyebrows, her feathery lashes.

She loved her face. She knew her face.

Margot traces the edge of her bandage, fingers curled like the narrow legs of a spider.

She knew her, once.

Who are you drawing, Margot?

How do you know her?

Where did she go?

THE NEXT MORNING, MARGOT TRIES to call her mother again.

A soft mist rises around the phone booth as she dials the nine digits. The phone bustles to life with a hum, and once again, Margot eyes the stone building on the hill. White fog hovers over the gargoyles, and she fights the temptation to scratch at her neck.

"Hello?"

"Mom." Margot rips her eyes away from the fortress. "It's me."

"Hello?"

"Can you hear me?"

"*Hel-lo*? Is anyone there?"

"Mom. Mom! It's Margot, it's—"

Her mother's sigh bursts through the receiver, and Margot thinks, without meaning to, of being small. Of her mother's warm breath on her cheek. Of rainstorms and hazy summer. Nostalgia scrapes at her veins.

"Mom?" she whispers.

"Stop calling here." Her mother only sounds pained. "Please."

The line clicks, and confused tears burn against Margot's lashes. For a moment, she rests her cheek against the metal box of the phone, pulse ringing.

Her mind flashes with an image of the red painting, resting on her desk back in her dorm. A stone of guilt forms in her belly.

Because Rowena wasn't the first face that came to her through the brushes.

The first was a boy named Benjamin. Margot was only five years old. She didn't know at the time. Didn't know that she was drawing a boy who was going to turn up blue at the bottom of a lake the following week with plum bruises on his neck. His name had been splashed across the papers for months: ***WHO KILLED BENJAMIN MOSS?***

Margot's mother was the only one who knew of that painting. When the news broke, she'd marched into Margot's bedroom, rummaged through her trunk of canvases. *We will never speak of this again*, she'd said, voice stormy.

But then there was Jessica. And Nathaniel. Genevieve. Wren, Thomas, Sam.

All of them, strangers' faces.

All of them, dead bodies.

Patrick. Kendall. Bobby.

Dead, dead, dead.

Oliver. Florence. And—

And beautiful, perfect Rowena Gibson.

Margot had painted Rowena on an April night when she couldn't sleep, and the next day, there she was. Strolling into her AP English class with a new student form, all wild copper hair and blazing azure eyes. Rowena Gibson was a poppy flower, a supernova, a girl plucked from another decade and dropped into the present. Margot had never seen anything like her.

And so she raced home from school that day to burn the painting she'd made the night before, desperate to believe that if she destroyed it, Rowena wouldn't die like all the others.

If she burned it, maybe they'd have more time.

A chorus of voices snags Margot's attention away from her thoughts. She rips her gaze to the throng of students outside the phone booth, all slinking toward the hill in the distance. A pair of broad hands splays on the glass in front of her, and she jumps before recognizing Adrian on the other side.

He presses his nose to the surface, the ghost of his smirk returning.

"P-Q," he calls. "You coming? Matriculation ceremony's about to start."

WHO KILLED BENJAMIN MOSS?
WHO KILLED BENJAMIN MOSS?
WHO KILLED BENJAMIN MOSS?
WHO
    KILLED
       ROWENA
         GIBSON?

THE STUDENTS HUDDLE IN A mass outside the fortress, an ocean of black cloaks. Margot shivers in the dew-laced air, pulling her own coat tighter around her.

"What happens now?" she whispers to Adrian.

"Headmistress decides if we're ready."

Standing on her tiptoes, Margot catches sight of Headmistress at the gates, a large black book cracked open in her palms. White fog swirls around her like smoke as she speaks with each student through a black lace veil hanging over her face.

Dread flattens inside Margot's belly. "Ready for what?"

"To start at your assigned post, P-Q." Adrian slides her a confused glance. "Have you been paying attention to *anything* since you arrived?"

"Post? What post?"

He gestures to the fortress. "Art majors are stationed here, on the main level. That's where the records room is."

"Records room?" Margot steps forward, fighting the urge to scratch at the bandage on her neck.

Adrian huffs a laugh, his breath spins silver in the September dawn. "Did you hit your head or something?"

He moves closer, high-top sneakers squelching in the mud, and brings his hand up to her forehead. His dark lashes flutter in a squint, and that familiar grin peels over his lips as his fingers curl into her hair.

Margot's cheeks burn, but she doesn't step back. Adrian's palm is warm against her scalp, and it reminds her of the way Rowena used to touch her. If she closes her eyes, she could almost convince herself it's Rowena's hand and not his, that they're standing in line for ice cream on the boardwalk, the coral summer sunset turning their skin to glitter.

They were supposed to have more time.

But then Adrian laughs, "I see the problem," and Margot snaps back to the foggy dawn. "There are spiders in your brain." He drops his hand, his shoulder lifts in a shrug. "It's common."

Margot heaves a sigh at the joke. "How do you get the telephone to work?"

Another smile. This one tinged with something resembling pity. "It only works after you've—"

"Mr. Vargas. Miss Percy-Quaid." Headmistress Prue's voice swallows his response. "*Silence.*"

Margot hadn't realized they'd moved this far ahead in the line.

"Mr. Vargas," Headmistress says again, and Adrian steps forward obediently. Headmistress studies something in the large book splayed open atop her palms, humming under her breath, before extending a weathered hand to tip Adrian's chin up to the bitter white sky. Margot watches with widened eyes as Headmistress tugs on his face, peeling back his lips to inspect his teeth, spreading his lashes wide. Finally, she nods, and Adrian starts toward the fortress.

"Wait," Margot calls.

He flings a glance over his shoulder. "I'll see you inside, P-Q."

The fog seems to engulf him as he walks the rest of the way, and an ache widens inside Margot's chest, carrying the fleeting idea that she may never see him again.

"Miss Percy-Quaid," Headmistress clips, and a bead of panic skitters along Margot's bones. "You aren't ready."

"What?" Margot breathes. "But you didn't—you didn't even look at me. Just now, you *examined* Adrian, picked at him like he was some kind of prize horse, but you didn't even—"

A hush falls over the crowd behind her. Without turning, Margot knows that her classmates' eyes must be rounded into little globes.

Headmistress, with her skeletal features and black veil, is not a woman you talk back to.

"I told you yesterday." Headmistress's voice is a darkened frost. "You have to bring me something new. *Paint* something new."

"I don't understand," Margot says, confusion barreling inside her.

"Miss Kensington," Headmistress chirps, and the girl behind Margot steps forward.

"No," Margot insists, but no one looks her way. "I want to go with Adrian, he was going to tell me how to get the phone to work. I have to call my mother. I want to go home, I—"

She slides her gaze toward the stone building. Adrenaline spins in her chest.

Before she can talk herself out of it, Margot sprints through the fog toward the gates of the fortress.

A burst of sound erupts behind her. Sudden, keening wind. Headmistress, growling her name. The other students, gasping like corpses into the stale morning air.

But she continues running running running, first through the mud and then along a slippery, leaf-covered path. The white fog embraces her, kissing her throat, her cheeks. Margot runs and runs, straight up the front steps, before tugging open the stone doors and disappearing into the shadows.

FOR A FEW MOMENTS, THERE'S only silence.

"Hello?" Margot whispers as she walks through a darkened corridor, blades of cold scraping her limbs. "Adrian?"

She turns corner after corner, but the building is empty. It's just her, the ashy shadows, and the echoes of her mud-drenched heels. She shouldn't have come in here.

But then, Margot blinks up at a door marked RECORDS ROOM.

She tugs the handle and steps through.

"Adrian—?!"

His name spills into a high-pitched gasp as Margot realizes that the floor has fully slipped away.

She's standing above an empty, cavernous pit.

"No-no," she cries, toes desperately curling to find her footing on the edge. The gaping blackness reaches up to her, yawning with hunger. Seconds away from a fall, Margot flails her hands in the dark, palms stinging as they make contact with something hard and narrow.

A ladder, she realizes with a surge of relief, clinging to it like a life raft.

Holding her breath, Margot dares a glance into the umbra below. She couldn't say for sure how deep the pit goes, but as her eyes adjust, she blinks her surroundings into view.

And bites down on a feral scream.

Because the walls are covered, *covered* in portraits.

Some are artfully crafted, watercolors bleeding on canvas. Others look like children's drawings—crayons and markers and construction paper. Stick figures and scribbles.

And beneath each painting, a name.

"What the fuck?" Margot breathes as she steps lower on the ladder, taking in name after name, face after face. "What the fuck, what the—"

But then, something halts her.

A drawing of a little boy beneath a black cloud. *Her* drawing. The first of the faces that Margot ever drew, when she was five years old.

Is he caught in a storm? Margot's mother had asked her that day, peering over her shoulder at the plastic easel.

No, she'd replied with a slow shake of knotted pigtails. *He's coming home.*

"Benjamin," Margot whispers now, heart hammering. Names and faces swim in front of her. Jessica and Sam and Oliver and—

"Adrian?" Margot gasps, chest aching at the sight of Adrian Vargas's face on canvas. His tan skin and dark eyes. His lips, forever frozen in a knowing smile.

But she doesn't have time to think of Adrian for long because her gaze lands on a painting of Rowena next.

Rowena. The painting she burned. It's right here, right fucking here in this pit. How—how the hell—?

And then, a wail of sorrow spills from Margot's lips as she sees the empty space next to Rowena.

The name that's written on the wall, with no picture attached.

Understanding slams into place. Dread cracks beneath her ribs.

Paint me something new, Headmistress had said. *Paint me something new.*

THEY WERE SUPPOSED TO HAVE more time, but all they had was a month.

One month of stolen kisses pressed against lockers, heat collecting between their palms. Rowena's copper hair like a starburst on the cotton of Margot's pillowcase, handheld walks through the poppy reserves on the outskirts of town. A flurry of text messages beneath blankets on nights they weren't together, the question of how it was possible to know someone for a few weeks and feel like you've known them your entire life.

Margot had burned the painting. She burned it, so nothing bad would happen.

They should have had more time.

She wishes she could remember more, but there are spiders in her brain. She's sure there was a rain-soaked July night. A streetlamp that was supposed to be lit. A deer that wobbled onto the road, yellow eyes like orbs in the night.

There were headlights. And then there was darkness. Something wet and warm against Margot's neck. A searing pain beneath her skull. And Rowena's hand, limp and cold in hers.

"It's going to be okay," Margot had whispered, words broken around the glass lodged in her throat from the windshield. "I'll find you in the poppy field tomorrow."

Her throat has been so very itchy since that day.

HEADMISTRESS PRUE'S OFFICE IS DARK when Margot enters, hands chapped with paint.

The older woman's voice slices through the shadows.

"Did you bring me a new painting?"

Margot nods and slides the canvas across the oak desk. She waits for Headmistress to look down at the drawing she spent all afternoon making.

A self-portrait, this time. All in black.

No color, no light.

"Very good," Headmistress purrs. "Let's hang it in its rightful place, Miss Percy-Quaid."

Margot touches the scars on her throat. They hum beneath her fingers. Glass shivers under her flesh.

A twisted spider's leg slips from her nostril.

Margot follows Headmistress out the door and tilts her face toward the white-bitten fog.

CONTRIBUTORS

MARIELLA ISABEL ACEVEDO is a third-generation Mexican-American born and raised in Aurora, Illinois, a Chicago suburb. She is a young aspiring writer and artist influenced by growing pains and dilemmas of the ever-evolving self. "Polyurethane" is her first publication and was produced during a year of study in New York City. Mariella plans to continue writing and expand her poetry collection (as long as she remembers to keep a pen on her). Find Mariella on IG at: @mariella.ace.

AARON H. ACEVES (he/him) is a bisexual, Mexican-American writer born and raised in East L.A. He graduated from Harvard College and received his MFA from Columbia University. His fiction has appeared in *Epiphany*, *The Florida Review*, and *Passages North*, among other places. He currently lives in Texas, where he serves as an Early Career Provost Fellow at UT Austin, and his debut young adult novel, *This Is Why They Hate Us*, was released by Simon & Schuster Books for Young Readers.

It received multiple starred reviews and was named a Best Young Adult Book of 2022 by *Kirkus Reviews*.

JOYA BREINHOLT is a second-year student at Wellesley College. Originally from Washington, DC, her writing focuses on themes of coming of age and womanhood with allegories of religion and politics. In her free time, she enjoys film photography, collecting perfume, and following Major League Baseball (Go Nats!). Find Joya on IG: @joya.breinholt.

ASHLEY DIERS is an illustrator and letterer. When not writing or creating art, she can be found searching local bookstores for her next favorite YA rom-com, exploring Minnesota's state parks, or drinking entirely too much iced chai, even in winter. She can also be found online at ashleyndiers.com or on Instagram/Twitter: @ashleyndiers.

DE ELIZABETH (she/her) is an author and journalist. She is currently an editor at *Parents*, and previously wrote for Netflix's editorial team. On the fiction side, she writes YA and adult horror, dark fantasy, and thrillers, and is represented by Root Literary. She is passionate about creating emotionally resonant dark stories with bisexual representation, and when she's not writing, she can usually be found drinking too much coffee and obsessing over morally gray villains. Find De on Instagram: @WordsByDe.

DYLAN FURBAY is a current high school senior in Bethesda, MD. He enjoys expressing himself through various creative outlets: writing, drawing, painting, piano. At school, he is proud to run cross country and track, edit for his school's literary journal, *Prometheus Unbound*, and help lead the Student Diversity Leadership and Pride Club. He is also the founder of youth litmag, *And Gallons*. Find *And Gallons* on twitter/X @ AndGallons. Read Dylan's work in *The Maze, Curio Cabinet, Uncharted Magazine, The Telling Room*, and *Poetry For Change*.

LIBBY L. KOWITZ (she/her) is a writer, bookstagrammer, and graphic designer from Cincinnati, Ohio. She is passionate about disability rights and representation in media and writes stories that center chronically ill and neurodiverse girls. When she isn't writing, she can be found drinking seasonal Starbucks coffees, tending to her (barely alive) plants, and collecting multiple editions of her favorite books. You can find her on Instagram: @ChronicAcademia.

EMILY SUN LI (she/her) is a Chinese American writer currently pursuing a dual MA in Children's Literature and MFA in Writing for Children at Simmons University in Boston, MA. Previously, she spent two years teaching English and studying Mandarin Chinese in Kaohsiung, Taiwan as a Fulbright scholar. Her experience in education started at the Taft School, where she served as an English Teaching Fellow as part of the University of Pennsylvania's Independent School Teaching Residency M.S.Ed program. She studied creative writing/English literature and environmental science at Emory University before graduating summa cum laude. Her poetry is published by *Button Poetry, Molecule*, and *Rigorous*, and her writing has been recognized by the YoungArts Foundation, *Voyage YA Journal*, and the City of Boston. When she's not reading or writing, she is probably procrasti-cleaning, drinking milk tea, or traveling with family and friends. Find Emily on Instagram: @poetry.by.e.

ELISA PARK is a Korean-American writer from southern California who has just returned from studying abroad in Seoul. She is delighted about the new emerging diverse voices in young adult fiction but feels that mental health has yet to be properly discussed in API novels. In the hopes that others can see themselves in her work, she is currently at work on her young adult manuscript. Find Elisa on Instagram at: @elise_ecit.

AMANDA THOMAS is an Indian-Australian fantasy writer, poet, and book blogger. She is soon to graduate from a Bachelor of Fine Arts (Creative Writing) at Queensland University of Technology, where she has studied as a Vice-Chancellor's Academic Scholar. Her work has been published or is upcoming in *Voiceworks, Blue Bottle Journal, Glass, Scratch That,* and Queer Sci Fi's flash fiction anthology *Migration* (2019). She has performed at several literary salons, including Volta Poetry run by the Queensland Poetry Festival.

LEAH NICOLE WHITCOMB is a proud Mississippian who writes about Black folks, love and magic. Her writing has been featured or is forthcoming in *Sistories, Samjoko Magazine, MadameNoire, The Rumpus,* and elsewhere. Leah co-hosts the *Hoodoo Plant Mamas* podcast. Find more of her work at leahnicolewhitcomb.com.

EDITORS

RACQUEL HENRY is a Trinidadian writer, editor, and writing coach with an MFA from Fairleigh Dickinson University. She spent six years as an English Professor and currently owns the writing studio, Writer's Atelier, in Maitland, FL. In 2010, Racquel co-founded *Black Fox Literary Magazine* where she is Editor in Chief and is the former Editor in Chief of *Voyage YA*. Since 2013, Racquel has presented and moderated panels at writing conferences, residencies, and private writing groups across the US. She is the author of *Holiday on Park, Letter to Santa, Christmas in Cardwick, Meet Me in December, The Write Gym Workbook*, and more. Racquel's fiction, poetry, and nonfiction has appeared in *Reaching Beyond the Saguaros: A Collaborative Prosimetric Travelogue* (Serving House Books, 2017), *We Can't Help It If We're From Florida* (Burrow Press, 2017), *Moko Caribbean Arts & Letters*, among others. When she's not writing, editing, or coaching writers, you can find her watching Hallmark Christmas movies.

MARQUITA HOCKADAY has a BA in history education, an MED in reading, a PhD in educational leadership, and an MFA in creative writing, which she earned from Fairleigh Dickinson University. After attending FDU, Marquita co-founded *Black Fox Literary Magazine*. She is currently Associate Editor at *Voyage*, a young adult literary journal. Marquita has done freelance developmental editing for fiction and nonfiction manuscripts, and, as an educator, she edits and provides feedback for academic papers. Marquita's short fiction is published in *Oyster River Pages* and *The Start Literary Journal*.

KIP WILSON is the author of young adult verse novels *White Rose* (Versify, 2019), about anti-Nazi political activist Sophie Scholl, *The Most Dazzling Girl in Berlin* (Versify, 2022), set in a queer club in Berlin during the last days of the Weimar Republic, and *One Last Shot* (Versify, 2023), about anti-fascist Spanish Civil War photojournalist Gerda Taro. Kip holds a Ph.D. in German Literature and is an Associate Editor at *Voyage YA*.

Special thanks to the *Voyage* readers:

Jena Brown

Robin Gow

Jeune Ji

Talia Moodley

Jenna Reasner

ABOUT VOYAGE YA
BY UNCHARTED

Voyage YA by Uncharted publishes short-form young adult literature. YA is an ever-expanding category of literature that constantly pushes boundaries. While the intended audience of YA is teenagers, almost half of YA readers are adults and *Voyage* is happy to be at the intersection of both groups. We are not interested in publishing a specific genre of YA, but we are interested in quality work by writers from a variety of backgrounds, especially #ownvoices. We are excited about creating a space that supports both emerging and established voices.

Find out more information about *Voyage YA by Uncharted* via our website: www.unchartedmag.com/genre/voyage-ya-by-uncharted/

Keep up with *Voyage* on our social media platforms:
Instagram: @voyageya
Facebook: facebook.com/voyageyajournal
Twitter: @voyage_ya
TikTok: @voyageya

A VOYAGE YA ANTHOLOGY
JUST
ABOVE
WATER
edited by Racquel Henry, Marquita
Hockaday, and Kip Wilson